# *Illusion*

## Joyce Johnson

**A Wings ePress, Inc.**
*Mystery Novel*

# Wings ePress, Inc.

Edited by: Jeanne Smith
Copy Edited by: Christie Kraemer
Executive Editor: Jeanne Smith
Cover Artist: Trisha FitzGerald-Jung

*All rights reserved*



Wings ePress Books
www.wingsepress.com

Copyright © 2020 by: Joyce Johnson
ISBN-13:  978-1-61309-574-4
ISBN-10: 1-61309-574-0

Published In the United States Of America

Wings ePress Inc.
3000 N. Rock Road
Newton, KS  67114

## *Dedication*


This story is dedicated to those kind ones
in my life who have helped me
attain my goal of writing books.

# **One**


A chance meeting can lead you down a different path.


Well, here I am, Matthew Handley, with quite the story to tell. I am a product of a marriage and dual parenting that ended with my mother's death early in my life. My father wasn't really equipped to be a single parent, or for that matter, a parent at all. I was left on my own a lot and I vowed to get good grades and make my way through college and beyond on my own merits.

After graduation, I married and hoped to start a family, but my wife wanted a career of her own. That career consisted of pushing me up an imaginary ladder she dreamed of ascending. We moved to the outskirts of San Francisco and I worked for a financial consulting firm. About five years ago, she gave up on my being a top executive and we divorced.

After the divorce, I chose to start a small business on my own in San Francisco and eke out an existence. I found a small apartment in the financial district and a shared office nearby. San Francisco is one of the most expensive cities in the country in which to live. It was a scary decision but exciting. When I wake up each morning in the city by the bay, I enjoy the beauty and excitement of the city and vow to stay.

The financial district is just one of the many unique districts in this small, compact city. San Francisco boasts about the oldest Chinese neighborhood in the United States, and Japan town, which occupies a much smaller space. We also have Russian Hill (without Russians), Nob Hill (sometimes called Snob Hill after the affluent citizens that built mansions on the hilltop of the city) as well as Haight-Asbury, Castro, and Fillmore districts which need little explanation. Even the Embarcadero with all its tourists excites me as I eat fresh crab on the street and look out onto the Pacific Ocean.

I have survived but not thrived in the city. As I used to remark to my ex-wife, who hated the phrase I made up and quoted to her almost daily, I might not own much, but my goal is not to owe much.

Each Friday, if I have a good week and, especially if I have a bad week in my tenuous job, I take myself out to my favorite restaurant for lunch. Located in the heart of the financial district and a short distance away from my office, the Old Tadich Grill has been at the same location for 160 years. It doesn't take reservations and didn't even accept credit cards until recently. Nevertheless, it is crowded each day with both locals, who consider it a favorite, and tourists who read about its reputation as a long-established must-visit.

The Old Tadich Grill brags about having the best seafood in town, which is something in a city with lots of establishments serving local fish and crab, especially those located along the seafront. Originally nothing more than a coffee stand in the Gold Rush days, the Grill has survived and maintains a historical flavor with stately male waiters in long white aprons. On one such Friday, I bumped into an old college friend, Steve, there by chance.

"What a coincidence," he said. "In all these years, I have never been to this old icon. After hearing about this place so many times, I decided I had better check it out. Didn't think I would know anyone here. Good to see you again, Matthew."

Steve looked the same. Still dashing, I thought, wearing a well-tailored suit that fit him perfectly. Still looks like the person who goes for the ring on the merry-go around. I always envied that attitude. I related this to myself as I brushed down my coat jacket, hoping it sleeked out the wrinkles from the off the rack suit I was wearing.

"Sushi restaurants are currently my favorite choice," Steve continued. "So what business are you in now, Matt?"

We sat at the long mahogany bar that was legendary and part of the charm of the old building. Because it was what Steve ordered, I broke my own rule and had a very expensive dry martini, even though beer was my favorite alcoholic drink.

"I left a large financial institution and started up my own company with some of the clients I worked with over the years, but I am always searching for new ones," I hinted.

Steve left that comment hanging and, instead, filled me in on the past years of his life.

"After my father died," he went on, "I inherited the construction company, and the business is doing well, despite my lack of interest. My wife, Anne, passed away from cancer only a year after my father died. I have remarried since and life goes on.

Despite tragedies in his life, Steve seems to be thriving. He did always seem to rise to the top.

I remembered when we were in college, where he majored in partying and I majored in accounting, he was easy going, relaxed, and always coming out ahead. Steve developed relationships easily and I enjoyed being around him and going to a few parties as his sidekick where he was the center of attention. We were in a couple of classes together and developed a friendship, although he really traveled in a different circle of acquaintances, one that had more money than I did. I hadn't seen or heard from him in years, but now, on this occasion, I got lucky with such a chance meeting. Maybe he can be a new client?

The maître d' called us to a table, and I ordered my usual Friday lunch, a steak sandwich, while he ordered a more expensive entrée, of course. I watched him with his impeccable manners and followed suit as best I could. After all, I needed to make a good impression if I ever hoped to secure him as one of my clients. Today would be a good day for reminiscing.

"Remember that old professor who always called me out for being late to his class?" Steve remarked.

"How can I forget? Who would believe such a short, skinny old man could have such thick veins in his neck that bulged out when he confronted you?"

Steve laughed so loudly the nearby customers stared for a moment. "And do you remember my reply?"

"Of course I do," I said. "You told him that you were so caught up reading the notes from his last lecture that it made you late. The whole class laughed."

"My father didn't think my grades were so funny," Steve said. "But with a full ride at school and lots of generous contributions from my father, I did make it through to graduation." Steve ordered a second martini from the waiter, but for reasons of my own, I declined.

"I need to leave straight way after lunch," Steve remarked, "because I have an important meeting, but this has been fun. Why don't you let me buy lunch for us at my favorite sushi restaurant next Friday and this time it will be my treat?" he asked, getting up from our finished lunch. I decided to take him up on his offer. The sushi restaurant is probably even more expensive than here, and maybe I can bring up possible business opportunities then.

With dollar signs swirling in my head, buoyed by a rekindled friendship with possible business advantages, I took one of my favorite walks back to my office before returning to work.

# *Two*

The following Friday, we met at an upscale, trendy sushi bar on Bush Street named Akido's. I'd heard of its reputation but never tried it because it was too expensive for my budget. Steve had insisted on going there and I, of course, agreed. After all, he was paying.

As we entered, the sushi chef was busy cutting up various fish, but as they always did in Japanese restaurants, he acknowledged our entrance with a greeting. I was not surprised, however, when the chef addressed Steve by name, asking if he wanted to order his usual meal.

We were seated immediately, even though there was a line waiting, and Steve and I were served cold sake and edamame right away. When the waiter arrived, Steve called him by name.

"This is a special occasion for us as long-lost college buddies. Please tell John he may choose whatever he wants to create for us."

The edamame was lightly salted, warm, and crisp, unlike some I had experienced at less expensive sushi restaurants in the city. The Japanese sake, although I usually ordered it hot, was unfiltered and creamy. I didn't reveal I had never enjoyed the likes of it, but inwardly decided to order it again sometime.

Cucumber salad has simple ingredients. Basically, it is comprised of sliced cucumbers marinated in a vinegar/soy sauce. I have tried it at home with little success. This salad was sublime. The cucumbers had to have been marinated for a while in a perfect sauce that made them slightly crunchy but smooth.

Next came the hamachi kama, which, according to the menu I had studied online before coming, was technically an appetizer. It was, however, a full tender cheek, actually the collar, of a yellow tail tuna and grilled to perfection. I picked at it carefully with my chopsticks, but I really just wanted to devour the whole thing.

My stomach was already full when they started bringing the main course. I hadn't eaten since the night before in anticipation of gorging myself. The sushi chef created a selection with the freshest fish I ever tasted, and I noticed there was no wasabi or soy presented to us.

Steve smiled. "Don't ask for any!" he warned me. "The chef would be very unhappy. He believes his sushi is flavorful enough without adding any condiments."

"Thanks for the warning, "I said as I looked over his shoulder and smiled at the chef behind the sushi bar.

I tried to finish all the food set before me, so as not to offend the watchful sushi chef. When we got the bill, Steve signed for it and excused himself to the restroom. I peeked at his receipt and noticed we had managed to ring up a four-hundred-dollar lunch bill. I was grateful I was not the one buying lunch.

Sometimes the people you know from college aren't the same at all when you encounter them years later, but Steve hadn't changed much. He was as gregarious and upbeat as when he was younger and seemed just as wealthy and ready to spend his money. At the restaurant, Steve casually introduced the idea of my visiting him the following weekend at his dad's old cabin in the small Sierra village of Sugar Pine. He had mentioned the cabin often in college, but I had never been invited.

"You haven't spoken to me about my being a client," Steve remarked. "Why not?"

"I assume you already have lots of financial advice from others," I said.

"Mostly old advisors from my father's days at the firm. I probably could use some new advice. Why don't you drive up to my cabin this weekend? Do you remember how to get there?"

He probably forgot I had never been invited when we were in college.

"Maybe we could talk about some possible business between us then?" he asked.

I promptly accepted and, as we left the restaurant, I was already thinking of some ideas to offer him the following weekend.

## *Three*

The following weekend, I found myself with the navigation application on my cellphone unmercifully droning on with directions to Pinecrest Lake in the Sierras. I belittled myself for leaving later from San Francisco than originally anticipated and enduring the weekend traffic out of the city. Crossing the Bay Bridge, I had to trudge with local commuters over to Interstate 80 to yet more interstate highways, but then I took a short exit to reach Highway 120, a much smaller road that would eventually get me to Sonora in the foothills of the Sierras.

Friday's commuter traffic is always horrible. I listened to my tapes and tried to imagine how wonderful the Sierras would be at the end of this supposed three-hour drive. Finally, when I reached Sonora, I had relaxed somewhat. I was driving through the foothills of the Sierra Mountains with grassy hills and scraggly oaks marking the area.

Sonora boasts an historic downtown reminiscent of the gold rush days of California. With a population of about 5,000 people year-round, its main street stores include boutiques and restaurants. I stopped for a latte at a trendy coffee shop whose interior was in stark contrast to the town's brick buildings and vintage facades.

Continuing past Sonora, I traversed through winding country roads, gaining altitude as I went. I was leaving the grassland chaparral and oaks as I climbed toward higher elevations. Pine trees came into view and greenness surrounded me. Now I was truly out of my urban environment. I was finally driving on Highway 108 which would take me directly into Sugar Pine with nearby Pinecrest Lake.

The smell of the pine trees and mountain air encased me, and I passed through picturesque-sounding small villages such as Twain-Harte, Mi-Wuk Village, and Long Barn, but didn't stop. I continued to the small Sierra town of Sugar Pine on the map Steve had scribbled on a cocktail napkin at the restaurant. It showed the turnoff from Highway 108 to Steve's cabin. When I arrived late toward evening, I noticed a black truck and Mercedes already parked in the circular driveway in front of the rustic cabin. I parked and, as I walked up to the front porch, I heard loud, quarreling voices coming from inside. Stunned, I paused, my knuckles within inches of knocking at the door.

"Why did you invite him, Steve? I thought just the two of us were going to discuss finances this weekend. He doesn't even work for a large financial company."

"We will...we will; be patient. There is plenty of time for that. Matt and I are only going to discuss my personal investments, but I also thought maybe he might just have some new good ideas for our business. After all, we can trust him, as we both knew him in college."

"Are you serious? It was you who was Matt's good friend in college, remember? I wasn't. I thought he was an outsider then, and I still think he is an outsider now...especially now!"

"Let's talk about this later. He'll be here any minute."

"No...now!"

"We have a guest arriving at any moment," Steve protested.

"I don't care. You invited him. Not me."

"For God's sake. Is it too much to ask you to be civil?"

My knuckles landed on the door with a resounding thud.

"There, see? Will you just shut up? He's already here!"

After I knocked at the door, the angry voices stopped. Then I heard footsteps, and a well-dressed man opened the door. He was wearing an expensive tailored, pin-striped suit which looked like the ones worn in the better financial offices in San Francisco. I thought we were supposed to dress in clothing more suitable to the outdoors, so I had worn jeans and a cotton shirt and brought a warm jacket for the colder nights.

I recognized him as being one of our college classmates by the name of Gordon. He sported thinning hair, an immaculate appearance, and a forced smile. Steve came up behind him and met me at the door, too, shaking my hand. Apparently, they didn't realize I had overheard them arguing.

"Come on in," said Steve, opening the door wider and placing himself in front of Gordon as I entered the room. "You remember Gordon from college, don't you? I don't know if I told you or not, but Gordon is my business partner."

I was surprised, to say the least. Somehow I thought Steve and I would be the only ones at the cabin that weekend. Steve had not mentioned Gordon, and certainly had forgotten to mention that Gordon was his business partner.

I looked around the living room at the interior of the cabin. It was built entirely from wood; I guessed it was originally constructed in the 1930s or 1940s. Even the curtains looked as though they were from that same period, with ruffles and tiebacks adding to that era of furnishings. There were lamps with dusty shades and a huge fireplace with antique bellows resting on the brick-laden hearth in front of it. The overall appearance was that of a cabin rarely used currently but filled with memories from the past. A few photos were inside the old wooden bookcase that housed lots of well-worn paperbacks.

"I guess it mustn't have been important and slipped your mind," I replied tight-lipped.

"Well, after I remarried, I decided to slow down a bit and share the business with a partner," Steve said, ignoring my biting sarcasm.

Gordon looked at Steve and I caught sight of his odd expression. I didn't think it was that simple. I assumed right away that Steve had needed an infusion of capital and wondered what else he had "forgotten" to tell me.

Steve proceeded to open a vintage wine. I noticed it was the second opened bottle, as there was an empty one on a nearby shelf. Even though I was apprehensive about the outcome of this weekend, I was determined to enjoy the wine. Somewhat later, Steve remarked he needed to get some supplies for dinner.

"Mind if I go into town?" asked Steve. "You just passed Sugar Pine on your way here...to pick up something for a late dinner. Everything there closes soon."

"Of course not," I replied. At this point, I preferred a talk with Steve or, better yet, I would prefer just traveling on up the road to a nearby motel, but I couldn't do that, at least not now. When I heard Steve's truck pull out of the driveway and head to town, I hoped what Steve meant by supplies was food and not more liquor. I hoped these two men were not heavy drinkers, and I was regretting my decision to stay. But tension was removed from the room as soon as Steve left. Gordon became more amiable, more astute about the construction business than I had previously assumed, and we actually had a decent conversation.

"Besides being Steve's partner in the construction business, are you involved in other things?" I asked.

"Oh yes," Gordon replied. "I'm in the export/import business in San Francisco. Mostly high-end antiques. It is a very lucrative business and over the years I've built up many good contacts. As you have probably already guessed, Steve needed more capital. I learned of that from his second wife, Nora. She and I have become good friends since their marriage. It was she who suggested I get involved in Steve's construction business as a somewhat silent partner," Gordon commented. I noticed his voice changed when he spoke the words, "silent partner."

Steve's time away from the cabin seemed to have eased the tension between Gordon and me, and when he walked in with a great-looking pizza and garlic bread, I was relieved. He offered me a soft drink, which I took as a good sign. As the evening progressed, Steve lit a fire. As it illuminated the cozy cabin, I relaxed completely. Maybe this weekend would not develop into a business prospect, but at least I could enjoy myself.

We sat up sharing stories from college. Gordon had not been part of Steve's bad behavior. Gordon had always been the studious, stern type, but their fathers were good friends and so they were somewhat obliged to be friends as well. Gordon even laughed at some of Steve's old practical jokes, but it was Gordon who first decided to call it a night.

"I think I'll make it a night also. It's just ten o'clock but I had a long drive," I said and got out of the comfortable leather easy chair I had succumbed to all night. I could have slept there near the disappearing embers, but I thought I should get a good night's sleep in a real bed.

I got up to leave when Steve whispered to me as Gordon disappeared down the hallway to his bedroom, "Let's talk more about you and me and our business prospects in the morning over coffee. Okay with you?"

"Sure, Steve," I replied, without much hope of that ever happening.

I asked which bedroom was mine for the weekend, and Steve mentioned the one at the far end of the hallway across from the one Gordon had just entered. It was a three-bedroom cabin with two bedrooms facing the front of the cabin near the road. My bedroom was facing the back, toward the lake. It looked as though Steve was staying in the living room for a while, leaving the chair he had been using and claiming the leather couch. I assumed he would probably sleep there, warmed by what was left of the fire and drink the remaining wine. Even in college, Steve had been a night owl.

Steve remarked out loud as I walked away, "Matt, don't worry if you hear me take a short walk out the back side of the cabin near the lake before I turn in. That's my regular routine," he said, "as it seems to relax me."

"Right on," I answered as I headed down the hall. I didn't even unpack my suitcase, but feeling tired, I lay down on the bed. Since my window looked out the back side of the cabin, the bright moonlight lit up my room and I wondered if I would be able to get to sleep. Reluctantly, I got up from the bed to close the heavy curtains. As I began closing them, I heard soft voices at first coming from outside Gordon's door. I guessed Steve had left his resting spot by the fire. I hadn't heard him coming down the hall to Gordon's room because of the thick carpeting.

Once more the two men got into an argument. I couldn't hear the words because at first the argument consisted of harsh whispers. When the whispers began rising to an angry tone, I became worried. I remembered those sounds from my childhood when my parents, returning from a party after drinking, would fight. I hated those memories of angry words and regretted being put in this position with two men I didn't really know anymore.

I looked at the small alarm clock on a table near my bed. It was the old, cheap kind that used to be found in chain drugstores, with its irritating red digital numbers indicating ten o'clock.

The voices grew louder and I could hear every word.

"Look at yourself, Steve," said Gordon. "You are a goddamn stumbling drunk! You even got the wrong bedroom! You opened my door, you fool!"

Slurring his words, Steve answered him. "Yeah, yeah. I know, I know."

"You know nothing," said Gordon. "Your business is in shambles and so is your happy home. Heard your wife has a lover."

"Ha! Maybe it's you," Steve accused back at him.

Then they both loudly hit the wall of my bedroom. I was about to go out and yell at them. This chance meeting I had taken as fortunate had turned into trouble. I cursed myself for getting involved with these boozers this weekend.

I heard Gordon say, "Just go to bed, Steve. You will probably not remember what I've said tomorrow." Gordon lowered his voice, so presumably I would be unable to overhear him. I stood next to the door with my ear peeled to the doorframe as I wanted to hear what Gordon said.

"Don't you dare hurt Nora again, or I will hurt you," Gordon threatened and, with that remark, shut his door. I heard the click of the lock. I went back to bed and promised myself I would wake up early the next morning and get out of this situation as fast as I could.

Just as my anxiety was decreasing, and I was finally getting back to sleep, I heard loud crashing noises outside my bedroom window. I got up, pulled the heavy curtains aside and saw Steve in his hiking boots and red plaid shirt walking down toward the lake, disappearing into the woods. Apparently in his drunken stupor, Steve had crashed into the garbage cans. A walk was not something I would undertake after drinking that much. I looked at the alarm clock again and this time it read midnight. I needed some sleep and closed the heavy curtains again to shut out the bright moonlight, but I couldn't dispel the image of Steve walking down to the lake at that hour. I finally fell asleep on top of the covers.

# *Four*

I overslept and awoke to a quiet cabin with the uneasy feeling of being in a strange bedroom. After orienting myself, I remembered the arguments of the night before and wanted out of this place as soon as possible. I was angry and tired and slammed back the heavy weighted curtains that had kept out the sunlight, causing me to oversleep.

Opening them revealed a bright, beautiful day, but the memory of two bickering partners spoiled it. Well, it was time to say goodbye and head for home. Hearing no voices or movement, I decided to head to the kitchen for coffee. After slipping on jeans and a shirt, I walked down the hallway to find Gordon sitting at the kitchen table.

He didn't look happy. I helped myself to some coffee. "Steve's gone," Gordon said simply.

"Well, I did hear you two arguing last night so I'm not surprised," I said.

He looked at me with a stern expression.

"No, I mean he's gone—he's not here—and I don't know where he is," Gordon replied.

As I looked out the living room bay window, I saw my car, as well as the black truck and the Mercedes, still there. I whimpered to myself, thinking any further complications with these two guys would indeed ruin my getting away early.

"Did Steve come back after you and he quarreled?

Gordon just stared at me.

"You probably couldn't hear it, but he kicked over the garbage cans walking away from the cabin at midnight," I said.

"No, apparently he didn't come back," Gordon replied.

"Have you called the sheriff?"

"For heaven's sake, no!"

"Well then, I will," I said getting up from the kitchen table. I wanted to scare him into taking some kind of action.

"Steve might get angry if we call the authorities," Gordon said, seemingly cooler than the night before.

"I really don't care," I replied.

"Don't! I don't think we need to," Gordon said. He was a big man and having witnessed his temper outburst, I thought it best to lower the anxiety level and come up with a compromise. Or I could just leave them to figure out their problems for themselves, but I didn't think I should.

"Let's look for him again before we call the sheriff. After all, Steve has done this before," said Gordon. "Steve has a lot on his mind lately. I'm sure he didn't fill you in on his circumstances, but it has been a difficult time in the business. The workload has decreased significantly, and Steve barely makes payroll each month, and that's with a reduction in the number of employees. It's not the same successful business his father began."

I found it difficult to sympathize with my two old college buddies. I hadn't inherited a family business, nor had I started out with having money like Gordon. I had carved out a niche for myself. There were no free rides for me. Gordon should have known Steve was not at all like his father and checked out the business before investing his capital. Steve's father put his life into his work and developed his business over many years, and besides, I didn't want to hear about their problems. They didn't involve me.

"Why don't we make breakfast for all three of us and by the time Steve gets back from his morning walk, we can forget all about my involvement in your business and just enjoy the rest of the day," I said.

Gordon seemed relieved, nodded his head in silent approval and added, "Steve brought plenty of supplies and there is lots of food stocked away in the kitchen cabinets."

We talked little as we opened packages of bread and bacon and a carton of orange juice. I made another pot of coffee, and when Steve still hadn't appeared, the two of us sat at the kitchen table. We ate breakfast in silence, waiting for Steve to alleviate the tension with his appearance. As more time passed, even our long drawn out breakfast didn't produce Steve. We both were aware that at the end of our meal we would have to decide what to do next. I was angry with Steve for his disappearance and putting us through this ugly situation. After too many cups of coffee, I was through waiting.

"He has never disappeared this long before," said Gordon.

"Before?" I asked.

"Yes, he gets angry and then takes off. It is a bad habit of his."

I didn't want to bring up any more college memories at this time, but I did recall at college Steve often disappeared when something unpleasant was about to happen, things that would set him off, such as situations with his angry father, or an argument with a fraternity brother. One time, when Steve had told his father of a class failure, his dad had raged over the phone. Steve handled the situation by leaving school and his classes for two days without telling anyone where he was going. We never did learn where he had gone, but when he got back, his father didn't rage at him for a long time.

"Well," I said, "It is possible he could be in trouble or had an emergency. Does he have any medical problems?"

"Not that I know of, at least. But he could have hurt himself while out walking or had an accident of some kind. We don't even know if he ever came back last night, or went out again this morning," said Gordon.

That comment made me think. "Have you checked his bed?"

"Of course I did," said Gordon. "This morning when I went looking for him. I found his bed was made, but then he is a neat freak, as you well know, so I didn't make much of that. I walked all around the cabin and walked down the path to the lake at the dock. Then I looked all around both cabins next to this one. I was very thorough. And his truck is still parked out front, as you can see. All his keys are in his bedroom as well as his cell phone. It appears he didn't take anything with him except perhaps some money."

"Let's make some calls into town. Maybe he walked down there. We could check the local stores," I said.

"Okay," Gordon replied. "In the meantime, I will call his wife and see if he called her. He may have called from town last night. Then again, I don't want to worry her. Let's wait awhile before calling Nora."

"I meant to ask you about that. His first wife died from cancer. Was that Beth from college? They were big time college sweethearts. Everyone expected they would marry, including me," I said.

Gordon chuckled. "Heavens no!" he said. "Steve and Beth discovered after college what they had in common was having fun. They fought like cats and dogs after they graduated and finally broke off their engagement. Beth married a dentist with a practice in Marin, but she and Steve have remained friends and have stayed friends even after he married Nora. The four of them get together all the time."

Gordon walked over to the window in the kitchen looking out to the backside of the cabin and the path to the lake, as if hoping to see Steve walking up to greet us.

"I'll take a look outside for him since I haven't been out yet, and you can make phone calls. When I come back, if I haven't found him sulking near the lake, we can check each other's information and then call the sheriff in town. I hope we don't have to do that," I suggested.

"I'll show you the path," Gordon said. We both headed out the back door. I was getting anxious about Steve's whereabouts, and was not happy with the circumstances he had put me through, but I did enjoy the prospect of some mountain fresh air.

The trail was narrow, but well contoured by the people who had walked it before. On both sides were pines and firs and a few wildflowers. The ground around the trees was covered with a thick patch of pine needles. As the pine trees became dense, so did the patches of their fallen needles and there were more shadows and less light. Still, some sunlight streamed through the trees from the cloudless blue sky above, and I thought I might as well enjoy my walk. Whenever he returned from one of his walkouts at college, Steve always returned at least somewhat remorseful at his thoughtless actions. He probably would be there at the cabin when I returned, or else Gordon might locate him by telephone in town having a drink at the local bar.

*Five*

Walking was easy, and I understood why a person staying at the cabin would enjoy this path. Soon, I came to a clearing that opened to the lake and the dock. It was a small lake, and judging from viewing its circumference, I could probably walk this half of the entire loop trail in forty-five minutes, and I needed the time to clear my mind.

At the lake was a makeshift dock and platform where a boat was tied up. As I walked on the gentle slope to the dock, I looked back and spotted my bedroom window. This was the angle from which I had seen Steve leaving at midnight. As I looked out at the lake, clouds were passing over slowly, making shadows on the smooth surface. Up close I realized the dock was no more than a platform with heavy metal rings attached at the top. The dock floated on the lake and was tied to the trees with heavy rope. I looked at both sides and saw other docks similar for the other cabins except some had four or five rung ladders for kids to climb and dive off into the lake. If it hadn't been for those two angry men, I would be asking for a boat ride instead of looking for one of them.

"Yesterday, before you came, Steve and I took the motorboat out of the shed for the first time this year," Gordon had said earlier that morning. He had pointed to a small storage building on the side of the cabin. From the shore I could see across the lake. On the other side, on the north shore, there were also cabins, but they could only be reached by the trail or by boat. Steve had told me that all supplies, including building supplies and trash, were hauled back and forth, usually by boat. I respected their sense of privacy, but thought it was a terrible inconvenience as well.

At the time, I asked if the trail indeed looped all the way around the lake, and Gordon had replied that it did. It was only a short four-mile trail. I hoped Steve had not decided to walk around the lake after midnight, but it was possible. Looking back, I spotted lights in the neighboring cabin on the right. The cabin on the left seemed deserted, with deep piles of leaves and pine needles surrounding it. There was no boat at its dock. Some smaller boards had fallen from the old cabin and it looked like it needed much repair.

I had asked both men about the neighboring cabins the night before, and it was Gordon who told me the situation. One cabin had been occupied by a widower with four children.

"Sad," Gordon remarked, "The old man who owned it passed away, and his children are squabbling over the ownership. It is taking a long time to settle their differences. These cabins don't go up for sale often, and if they do, they are usually sold right away."

"What about the other cabin?" I asked.

"An old guy. Quite a character. Lives here full time. Keeps to himself mostly."

I wandered down the trail and marveled at the majesty of the setting. The lake lay in a small hollow between granite cliffs and towering pines. The water, as I ventured down to touch it, was icy cold. Its gray stillness was only disturbed by me, a passing small fishing boat, and two ducks skimming the small bays for food.

They disappeared as I resumed walking the trail, enjoying the wind created waves lapping the shore. The wind was light and blew through the leaves of the trees. It was a quiet setting as the clouds wandered by creating shadows from time to time. For a Midwesterner like me, it was enchanting. Spring was short there followed by humid summers with the stillness indicating drenching heat. Here, the light wind made for a pleasant spring day and I could imagine a pleasant summer. Remembering my current circumstances marred the experience.

"Steve...Steve!" I called out at intervals as I walked, and I spent about an hour or so discovering my way around this secluded lake. My feelings alternated between worry and anger. Occasionally, I worried about finding him on the back side of a boulder or slumped on the ground at the next turn in the trail, the victim of a fall or a heart attack. But I tried to keep those thoughts at the back of my mind. I preferred anger to worry.

Halfway around the lake, I came across an uphill section. Large granite boulders made the climb somewhat difficult, but I was rewarded with a splendid view and a glimpse of a small dam, previously obscured from view. The trail crossed over the spillway, and I worried Steve might have walked across the spillway in the dark, fallen, and was lying sprawled at the bottom of the dam. I got my nerve up and looked over, but I didn't see much but some jammed up logs and garbage. Steve was nowhere in sight. I retreated back to the cabin and I hoped to be relieved of this anxiety by news of his being found. I would rebuke him for being thoughtless.

As I walked up from the lake to the cabin, I checked around front and saw all our vehicles still parked in the driveway. I heard no conversation as I opened the door, and much to my regret, I found Gordon by himself lying on the couch indulging in an early beer. I asked the question for which I already knew the answer. "Have you located Steve?"

"No Steve anywhere. I asked all over town. No one has seen him since his visit last night. I called the restaurant, the bar, the tackle shop, even the hardware store. No one has seen him this morning. They saw him last night when he got the pizza, but not this morning. As a last resort, I even called the sheriff." I thought Gordon was supposed to wait until I returned to call the sheriff, but I let his oversight pass.

"The sheriff said he would make a few calls—cover those areas I may have missed. He hoped you might find him contemplating his financial woes on a boulder at the lake."

"I think it's time you called Steve's wife," I said.

"You're right," Gordon replied. He walked to the kitchen and picked up the land phone.

"I hoped Steve had called Nora. I can't believe he would put her through this worry as well," I said.

I watched as Gordon talked in short, muted sentences with someone on the other end of the phone. I tried to give them some privacy but was curious as to the conversation. I only heard bits and pieces of what Gordon said.

"I'm sure...show up."

"How's...been acting..."

"What...more business concerns..."

I heard a jeep pulling up to the cabin, screeching to a stop in the gravel of the driveway. From the window, I saw the sheriff making his way to the door.

"Good morning, Sheriff Thompson, I mean Frank," said Gordon, extending his hand. "Sorry to bother you again."

"Again?" I said out loud. "What do you mean again?"

No one answered my question.

"No problem. It's my job. What is it this time, Gordon?" Thompson asked.

"We can't find Steve. He may have walked away from the cabin sometime in the early hours of the morning. We don't know for sure, but we can't find him."

"And who is this?" asked the sheriff, nodding his head toward me.

"His name is Matthew Handley. Steve invited him up here this weekend supposedly, according to Steve, for a possible job."

"I thought his company was having business problems lately," Frank replied.

Seems like everybody except me is aware of that fact.

"Well, you know Steve. Always the optimist," Gordon replied.

The sheriff wanted to take a quick look inside the cabin and outside. I stayed inside asking myself a number of things.

Why hadn't Steve just taken his truck? What did Frank mean about 'this time?' Where had Steve gone before? Most importantly, could we find Steve soon so I could just go home and salvage the rest of the weekend and my sanity? The sheriff seemed competent and not too worried.

While the lawman was outside looking around, Gordon said, "Sheriff Thompson says we should stay here another night in case Steve should call. If he doesn't show up, Frank wants us to stop by his office before leaving town. He has some forms for us to fill out, including telephone numbers where he can reach us, that sort of thing. But Frank is hoping this whole situation will resolve itself before that."

I sighed to myself when Thompson finally drove away. I was not happy to remain here at the cabin, but it was a practical suggestion in the rare chance Steve might call, and besides, we needed to know Steve was safe.

Gordon and I discussed having an early dinner as neither of us had eaten since breakfast. It would not be wise for us to eat out since at least one of us needed to stay near the phone and the cabin, and neither of us wanted to eat alone in the town. Too many questions. By then, everyone in town most likely had learned of the situation. So we decided to scrounge up something to eat from the pantry.

I am not much of a cook and eat out much too often. Gordon seemed to be exactly the same type of single person, so we ate some of the food Steve had brought back from town. Dining on grilled cheese sandwiches and tomato soup was good enough for us. We ate with little conversation between us, as we had little in common except our mutual friend. Steve was our only link, and he was missing.

After dinner, we sat in the living room and discussed a little about Steve's personal finances and his emotional state. But Steve's partner didn't want to reveal a lot about either, and I really didn't want to hear it. Finally, we both retreated to our separate rooms for privacy.

I read my neglected novel for a short time but turned off the light when I couldn't concentrate. Getting to sleep was not easy. I kept waiting for a phone call, hopefully from Steve. I finally dozed off to a dream about the lake which was illuminated by a full moon. The dream featured me looking for Steve.

<h1 style="text-align:center">Six</h1>

I awoke the following morning at seven o'clock, having set the alarm the night before. I fumbled to turn it off and wondered if Gordon was already awake. It took several minutes for the depression of the night before to set in. I found Gordon in the kitchen making coffee. We didn't need to discuss the day before or the obvious lack of news. Our only discussion would be how to get out of town and when.

A few minutes later, Sheriff Thompson drove up with a young deputy in tow. He advised us that he started a search party around the lake, which had begun even earlier that morning.

The phone rang and I answered it. There was a woman on the other end of the line asking for Frank.

"I handed the land phone over to him and only heard his end of the conversation punctuated by short answers like okay."

He hung up. "That was Julie," said Frank, "she works in my office."

"What did she say?" I asked.

"She said...she said they found Steve," Frank said slowly. "I mean they found his body in the log jam below the spillway at the dam."

"No, oh no!" yelled Gordon. "We have to call Nora right away. She needs to know. She needs to know."

"Hold on," said Frank, who was clearly in charge. "Let's wait until we can give her more detailed information."

I looked over at the young deputy who appeared stunned.

"Biggest thing I was ever involved with before was a helicopter rescue for an older hiker who experienced a heart attack. This is really something!" the young deputy cried out.

The sheriff scowled at him.

"Pull yourself together and have Julie call the coroner right away. As for you two," Frank said pointing to Gordon and me. "You can come with me to the dam. The coroner can meet us there to decide where we should take the body and whether we should take it to the next town for an autopsy. We'll go in my jeep."

Before I could register a response, I found myself in the back seat of the sheriff's jeep with Gordon, heading for the dam. I wasn't anxious to see a dead body, but Frank seemed eager, judging by the speed in which he maneuvered the turns.

We drove on a service road to the back of the dam where next to the spillway there was a vacant lot used for service and emergency vehicles. The dam spillway was small—no more than thirty feet wide with a metal bridgeway crossing over leading to the foot walkway. It was this walkway I had crossed earlier and peered down the spillway. But I didn't have this close a view or angle earlier.

A buoy line—looking like a purse seine net—encircled a small area in front of the spillway, trapping tourist garbage, including empty water bottles, forgotten or lost shoes, and Steve's body floating in the middle trapped by a couple of stray and broken tree limbs. As we approached the turnout parking area, I spotted a maintenance truck parked next to a small storage shed. I assumed the shed held the gauges needing to be checked, as well as various tools. Two men were looking where Steve's body was floating, pointing and gesturing as if deciding what to do. I hoped they would have retrieved Steve before we arrived, but they had not. Sheriff Thompson drove his vehicle close to where the men were standing and stopped. He got out first and walked up to the men while we were still scrambling out.

"Bill, why didn't you get the body out?" he asked one of them.

"Left that up to you, Sheriff. Thought you might want to see it first. We can't agree on how to retrieve it anyway."

Since the coroner had not arrived, we walked to the edge of the dam where all eyes were focused on the body. Looking more closely, I could make out the same red plaid shirt I had seen Steve wearing. Garbage was floating all around him.

"What's your idea about getting him out?" asked Bill.

"Pull him out," Gordon said, as if talking to a child. "Treat the body like a tree limb but be gentle as possible without damaging too much."

The men used the same long hooked pole they used to pull out logs and tree trunks and tugged at Steve's clothing until they cleared him along with a smaller tree trunk. The coroner arrived as we were pulling Steve's body out of the spillway. A helicopter was landing on level ground nearby, and I assumed it would take the body for an autopsy at a larger, nearby town.

Having only seen one dead body before this—that of my great-uncle at his funeral when I was ten years old—I stood mesmerized and virtually useless. I leaned against the sheriff's jeep hoping this nightmare would end soon as I just wanted to return to the city. As the helicopter rose out of sight and the coroner drove away, I decided to take the opportunity to say goodbye.

"Well, Frank, I would appreciate a ride back to my car. Not to be insensitive, but I can be of no further help. I want to start driving back to the city before it gets dark. I will leave you my cell phone number, so you can call if I can be of any further help," I offered.

"Not so fast. I need you to stay tonight. I want to ask you some questions, and I would rather do that in person than on the phone. It would be better to discuss this incident while the details are fresh in your memory. Most likely it was an accident," Frank offered.

"Of course it was an accident," I said.

I really did not want to stay another night, especially with Gordon in the cabin. It was getting dark and I was tired and upset. Perhaps I can stay at the inn I saw across the road and leave in the morning after talking with Frank. I could eat something, take a hot shower, and get a good night's sleep.

"If I must stay here in Sugar Pine, I don't want to stay at the cabin. Do you recommend the Sugar Pine Inn across the highway? I didn't get much sleep last night."

"You didn't get much sleep at the cabin?" Frank asked, looking into my face. "Why not?"

"Well, the partners were arguing about business. I don't think it had anything to do with this unfortunate accident, except that it is probably why Steve took a walk at midnight," I said.

Sheriff Thompson did not reply for a few moments. I already felt I had said too much, but then again, I would say the same thing tomorrow morning.

"Steve always had his problems," Frank muttered under his breath. "To answer your question, The Sugar Pine Inn has nice rooms, cheaper than the lodge at the lake. I never stayed at either place myself, but Julie recommends the inn to visitors. You can come to my office in the morning. I'll tell Gordon to ride back to the cabin with Bill now and Gordon can come in later to see me as well."

I nodded, glad for a place other than the cabin to spend the night and rode with the sheriff solemnly to the cabin to get my car. I was stunned by the day's events and didn't want to discuss them anymore with Gordon.

Frank left me at the cabin with a not so gentle reminder. "I'll see you first thing tomorrow morning," he warned from the jeep's window before he drove off.

I entered the cabin through the sliding back door which I knew we had left open and went to the bedroom. I packed my stuff and left a short, written message by the cabin phone for Gordon. I assumed Gordon didn't really want to see me again either.

Driving away was one of the hardest things I'd ever done.

## *Seven*

The next morning after a restless night at the inn, I drove to report to the sheriff. The few buildings along the highway in town were strung out, except for one small, white wooden building with a large bold sign proclaiming SHERIFF printed in capital letters on the front with a sheriff's insignia in gold next to it. The building was located by itself at the end of the street. Julie turned out to be the youthful sounding woman on the phone who had called at the cabin.

She was short and slim with long brunette hair pulled away from her face.

"I am much calmer now," Julie explained. "I am trying to get things organized. Nothing like this ever happens here."

I could see Frank in his office on the computer, but Julie said I could just walk in. Frank sat me down in his small office and started asking questions right away. No small talk.

"How long have you known Gordon?" the sheriff asked.

"I knew him slightly from college, but hadn't seen him in years," I replied.

"Then why were you staying at the cabin with him?"

"You didn't let me finish," I said.

This conversation was getting off to a bad start. I felt as if I were being interrogated, but I decided to change my tone. I sat up straight and told him the whole story from the beginning.

"So you knew them both from college, but you knew Steve more as a friend?" asked the sheriff.

"Yes, and as I said earlier, the two of them seemed to be quarreling about business."

"And you didn't join in any argument. Is that right?" Frank asked.

"Correct."

"So you saw Steve leaving the cabin at midnight. You looked at the clock because you were awakened by the garbage cans being turned over. And let me get this clear. You made no attempt to stop him, although it was very late, and Steve had been drinking. Is that a correct statement?"

"I made no attempt to stop him. That is correct. Steve is…was, I mean, a grown man. Perhaps during the weekend we might have decided to do some business together. Steve and Gordon had been arguing, and I assumed Steve needed some fresh air. Steve had been drinking quite a lot. Why don't you ask Gordon these questions?"

"I will," said Frank, "especially about the arguing. In the meantime, I'll have Julie type up your statement—what you said. You can sign it in the morning before leaving for San Francisco. I may have more questions for you by then."

"I don't want to stay another night, Sheriff," I lamented.

"Sorry about that, but I have a lot for Julie to do today. She will get on it as soon as she can," Frank said solemnly. "It's a small office."

"Please tell Julie I will be here promptly at nine o'clock," I said as I got up and walked to the reception area.

I felt sorry for Julie, but I wanted to leave town first thing in the morning. Now I wished I had not been so cooperative and just driven home instead. I was exhausted, and I just wanted to sleep in my own bed.

On my way out, I noticed framed photos hanging on the wall. They were of the local area and photos of events in the little town. One in particular caught my attention. I stopped for a moment and looked closer. In the photo were three fishermen—Steve, Gordon, and Frank, each holding a large fish and sporting big grins on their faces. Then Frank stepped out of his office and came up behind me.

"Nice photo," I said. "So you and Steve fished together. How long have you been friends?"

"Steve and I were friends when both of us were young during summers when his parents came to their cabin. After they died, Steve kept the cabin and has been coming here occasionally ever since."

I nodded and closed the door behind me on the way out of his office. Why was Frank keeping this information to himself?

# *Eight*

I drove back the few miles to the Sugar Pine Inn and checked into my room. I ate outside on the open porch in a pleasant shaded area with a few other tourists, as the season had not officially opened. Everyone was courteous and helpful as I was the only customer.

The waiter was a friendly young man named Kit who spent his winters teaching skiing at the small ski area up the highway, Dodge Ridge, and his spring and summers working as a waiter and a bartender at the inn. Kit had heard about the incident and, since I was the only customer, he assumed I was involved.

I gave him a brief account and told him of my walk halfway around the lake. Kit said it was a usual tourist hike because the trail was mostly level especially on the east and west shores and a quiet way to enjoy the lake. The entire loop trail was only four miles long, and I had only walked less than half, from the cabin to the dam and back. It was early, and I didn't want to watch television or read the novel I had brought. Instead I decided to walk across the highway toward a beach at the end of the lake.

It lay at the south end of the lake, less than halfway from the dam. Not tourist season yet, it was almost deserted. From this point of view, the tourists could see the full extent of the lake and the swimming area marked with colorful buoys. Adjacent was a dock where small sailboats and paddle boats were rented. They were all tied up for possible use behind a sign advertising them. The whole area at the back of the sandy beach was covered with various pines and firs, creating a scenic setting for the small campground located there. On one side of the beach was the lodge which I had not investigated. It was altogether a peaceful scene if one wasn't aware of the tragedy.

A covey of small shops was at the lodge: a bait shop, souvenir shop, coffee shop, post office and a small grocery store. According to the grocery clerk who gave me directions to the trailhead, the big lodge built for tourists during the boom times of the logging days was razed by fire in the 1980s. The building had not been rebuilt as a lodge. Now it was only possible to rent motel rooms or stay at the campground. A small bar and some offices were located on the second floor.

Steve told me this recent fire had renewed an ongoing feud among the owners of the private cabins around the perimeter of the lake such as he, whose property lay on National Forest sites, and the National Forest Service who sought public control. Private owners worried whether the NFS would allow them to rebuild their homes if they lost them in a fire. The fact the powers at the NFS hadn't allowed the old hotel to be rebuilt completely caused further anxiety and dissension between the two opposing sides. The dispute had calmed down in recent years but grumbling and animosity continued to a certain extent to the present. So much for a tranquil paradise.

The clerk confirmed north shore cabins could only be reached by foot or by boat—a concept I still found hard to believe. Answering my questions, he said the garbage from those cabins was collected weekly by boat and if cabin owners did repair work on their properties they had to haul paint and lumber the same way...by boat.

It was an easy, short walk to the well-marked trailhead by the boat rentals. The trailhead was snuggled between another service road to the dam and the small marina where the kayaks, motorboats, and paddleboats waited for customers. There were many ways to enjoy being on the lake. It certainly seemed a hot spot for the tourist season that was about to begin. I spotted two kayakers coming ashore. This was the end or the beginning of the loop trail around the lake, and since I had not gone this far looking for Steve, I had not been on this part of the walk.

The path was gentle and easy, passing by cabins that looked very similar—wood construction, mostly unpainted, and outside porches. Most were one story cabins, with a few two stories high with the lower level used as a winter shed, locked and shuttered. Each bore a cute name devised by the owners or the names of the owners themselves—Bird's View, The Mattelsons, Patterson Family Hideaway. Some displayed aspects of individuality such as painted flowers on the shutters or a distinctive flag, but they blended together as if there were restrictions for looking alike. Every so often a hiker or two would pass me on the trail coming or going.

Soon I found myself coming to the area of Steve's cabin. The sight of it sent a small shiver through me. I looked up to see the familiar lights of the cabin to the right, but instead it was dark inside. The cabin on the left somehow took on a sinister look. I hoped another hiker would be approaching soon to dispel this uneasy feeling coming over me. I decided the only way to conquer my fear was to face it head on, so I looked more closely at the deserted cabin.

There was a light in the cottage to the left of Steve's cabin walking away from the lake. I decided to visit its occupant and walked boldly up to the front porch which faced the lake. I noticed the front door was open, but since it was becoming dark, I thought perhaps I should call it a day. It was warm especially for this time of year. So I knocked lightly, but no one appeared. I am not sure why I entered the cabin. I suppose I could say if approached about entering I was worried the cabin had been burglarized or someone needed help. The truth was I was just curious.

The décor in the interior of the cabin seemed stuck in the era in which it was built—probably the 1940s. All the furniture was dark and heavy and looked hand cut, as if the owner had constructed them from nearby trees. The usual parchment lamps were not lit, and I had difficulty finding my way around the room. I saw a faint light coming from a back bedroom and used it to guide me towards its source. I should have turned back, at that time, but like a moth drawn to a flame, I just kept going.

In my defense, I tried to announce myself by calling out in a medium loud voice, as not to sound frantic. "Hello. I'm a neighbor. Is anyone there?"

I don't know why I cupped my hands over my mouth when I uttered these short sentences, but I felt like an actor in a B horror movie, certainly not myself. I shouldn't be here.

I heard someone stand up from a squeaky bed in the back room and the noise sent shivers down my spine. I tried to back out of the cabin quietly, but I heard footsteps coming toward me. I was caught and before I had a chance to run out the front door, I stumbled backwards over a chair leg and fell on the floor. My presence was revealed before I could get out of the darkened cabin. Standing over me with ear buds hanging from his youthful body, was someone in his early twenties or late teens with a startled expression on his face.

"Who are you?" he asked as I struggled to regain my composure and stand to face him squarely.

"Your neighbor," I said. "I guess you didn't hear me with your headphones plugged in. The door was left open and I thought someone might need help." It seemed a lame excuse even to me.

"Everyone who owns cabins here seems to be as old as the cabins themselves!" I protested.

"You are right on that point," he laughed. "You startled me. My name is Pete." Then I introduced myself and we shook hands properly.

"My grandfather and grandmother owned this cabin. They built it by hand a long time ago," Pete continued. "Nothing has changed much since then. When my grandparents passed away, my parents just couldn't get motivated to sell it. Then my siblings started bickering over the proceeds and how the profits would be divided. They are still squabbling about it and so it just sits here, mostly deserted."

Pete walked over to the side table by the well-worn couch and switched on the light. "You said you are my neighbor?" Pete questioned.

"Yes," I replied. "I am staying at Steve's cabin. He disappeared while I was staying there. I still can't believe how he died."

"Me too," Pete replied.

"Were you here that night?" I asked.

"No, I just came today and heard about it when I got some groceries in the village. The gossip crew has it that he drowned, but they seem somewhat skeptical," Pete answered.

"Of what?"

"Just skeptical. Around these parts local gossip is about all there is to do. Steve's death was big news and wild points of view are being conjured up."

"Like what?"

"Well, for one Steve's wife's brother, Bobby, has always been in trouble. He lives way up the highway and talk around town is he has bought and sold drugs, besides using them himself. I have even purchased some drugs from him myself," Pete remarked almost proudly and as if to prove his point lit up a joint.

"Do your parents come here often?" I asked.

"No," Pete answered. "Just me. I am supposed to look after the place when I come up." He laughed at the last remark. The place looks unkempt. I don't think he works hard at maintaining it.

"I have seen couples coming up here over the years and stay at Steve's cabin. They don't always come with the same partner, if you get my drift."

"I do. Any late-night swims or accidents involving boating?" I asked.

"Never. I never witnessed any visitors take that old boat out on the lake. That's one of the reasons why I was so surprised at Steve's drowning. Steve told me once he didn't know how to swim. And the so-called accident happened at night in the lake. That doesn't sound like something he'd do."

"Don't want to keep you from listening to your music," I said and started for the door.

"Heard at least one person speculate it could be murder," Pete stated flatly.

I turned back toward him and asked, "Why? Why do they say that?"

"Just seems mysterious, I guess," Pete offered as he headed back to the bedroom where his comfortable bed awaited him. "All sorts of suspects. His business partner, his wife, a lover, maybe even his wife's brother, Bobby. Couldn't prove it, though. After all, Steve drowned."

"Yes, Steve did drown," I muttered to myself as I walked out the door and shut it behind me.

I had enough of this lake and its cabins for one day and got back to the inn just as my stomach growled for dinner, glad for my own company.

~ * ~

Sheriff Thompson and I made peace the next day. The statement was ready to sign, and Frank's tone and demeanor had changed. He apologized for his attitude at the time of the accident. He was in shock and took the tragic event out on me, a stranger. Rambling on about their friendship, Frank made it clear he genuinely liked Steve. He provided little anecdotes about their fishing incidents together that reminded me of the good times I shared with Steve. In fact, the sheriff seemed more interested in talking about his memories of Steve rather than the circumstances of his death, but I persuaded him to reveal the findings of the autopsy. He said the autopsy was clear cut. Steve had drowned. He had no other cause of death, such as heart failure or a stroke. There were no cuts or bruises on him, so they didn't think he had fallen into the dam spillway from the trail. There was some marijuana found in his blood, and I was surprised Steve had kept that college habit. No life jacket or boat was found at the scene. It was still a mystery exactly how the accident had happened.

At the end of our conversation, Sheriff Thompson indicated he would appreciate my attending the funeral as he couldn't. It would be a short service at a funeral chapel, followed by a reception at the house in Marin. At a later date, Steve's ashes would be interred privately. The sheriff had spoken with Nora, and I was welcome at the house, but I had already decided to make a quick appearance at the service and skip the rest.

# Nine

When I entered the funeral home, I remembered one of the reasons I avoided them. The music was grim, the colors drab, and the flowers gave off a sickeningly sweet odor only found in funeral homes. The whole effect was oppressive. I reminded myself I wanted no such event for myself. I signed the guest list for myself and Frank and chose a seat inside the chapel near the door for an early exit if possible.

I knew almost no one in attendance. It was a blending of persons I would probably never see again. The minister spoke about Steve in generic terms and I doubted he ever met him while he was living. Gordon and Steve's sister then spoke kindly about Steve's life, and then mercifully the service concluded.

As I walked out of the chapel into the small lobby at the front, I noticed a small group huddled together. I recognized Gordon at the center and decided to at least make him aware of my presence since I wasn't sure anybody ever read the guest log.

As I approached, they were engaged in animated conversation. One woman in expensive clothing conveyed an air of wealth, so

I decided she must be Nora. A man standing next to Gordon was possibly their lawyer, as he looked like one. I was more curious about the couple standing with them. The woman stared at me and then I recognized Beth, Steve's girlfriend from college, although the years had not treated her kindly. Her face looked tense and strained, lined with fine wrinkles that stretched across. She dressed conservatively, and her appearance conveyed someone who dressed with little care. The man standing next to her, I presumed was her husband, looked about her age and kept shifting his weight back and forth—first one foot and then the other in an impatient motion. I understood that feeling. I didn't want to interrupt, but when Gordon spotted me, he turned and waved at me in acknowledgement. He immediately introduced me to Steve's wife, Nora.

"It was nice of you to come. The sheriff—Frank—sent his regrets. I do apologize for the inconveniences our affairs have caused you," she said.

"I only regret I wasn't any help," I answered.

"Please," Nora said, "Do come over to the house for the reception. I would like to speak with you further if I may."

"That's very kind," I replied. "I really hadn't intended to be there."

"Oh, but you must come," she said. "Excuse me. I see people I need to talk with that won't be able to come to the house. I look forward to talking with you further." Nora strolled off, since everything was settled. Obviously, she was used to having her own way. So I dutifully drove to Steve's house in Marin, wondering why I had agreed. I called Marin an unofficial suburb of San Francisco, but you would never hear that description from anyone in either area.

I pulled my car into the circular driveway outside the house, and a valet took it somewhere. At this point, I didn't care where. I was glad I found the house so easily. Located high in the hills of Marin outside of San Francisco, it stood out by itself, even among all the expensive houses on the way up to its location. Steve's house reflected the life style I supposed for him after college. It was an impressive house with an even more impressive view. If Steve had financial problems, this house could be part of the problem.

A maid answered the door, and I stepped inside to the foyer. To the right was a massive living room swathed in soft cream colors and immaculate, as though no one lived there. The maid pointed to the living room, even though it was obvious where everyone was congregating.

When I entered, I noticed more guests overflowing into the adjoining den and hallways. It seemed more people wanted to attend the party than the ceremony itself. There were about sixty people mingling throughout, carrying wine glasses.

I wandered through the house, more curious about its contents than the guests. Entering the spacious kitchen, I found myself eavesdropping on a conversation, or rather an argument between the caterers and the mistress of the house. It was obvious Nora was in charge and accustomed to that position. As I didn't want to intrude, I continued down the hallway where, once again, I found myself eavesdropping. This time it was between two women. As I continued walking I couldn't help but overhear a few comments.

"The man just couldn't manage money, that's all," one said.

"Now he doesn't have to worry. She will manage it all!" said the other. Both women began snickering and I decided my tour was over. I walked back through the kitchen to where I last saw Nora, hoping to speak with her, but she had already left and only the caterers remained, mumbling among themselves. I decided she had returned to her guests in the living room and headed in that direction. I spotted her in a group, but recognized someone I knew first and went over to speak with him.

"I didn't expect to see you here," I said.

"I didn't expect you here either," he countered. "What kind of business are you in now?" he asked. "Was Steve a client of yours?"

"I have my own financial consulting firm." I said. No need in revealing it is a shared office with a shared secretary. "I hadn't seen Steve in years. We were just discussing maybe doing some business together."

"I heard the construction company his father owned was not doing well. Not a matter of no housing construction right now, more of a lack of business management. Grasping at straws at the end... grasping at straws," he said.

"I don't understand what you mean," I replied.

"You don't get the big picture. At the end, Steve was asking everyone for help, and it was becoming embarrassing. You were only one of many. The man was sinking amid his and his wife's spending. The construction business does have its ups and downs, but Steve didn't build up his resources for when it went down. He was not as shrewd a businessman as his father. Steve's accident or suicide or whatever it was, really surprised me though. Bad luck! He always used to come out a winner, no matter what."

I always thought that, too. Maybe I was just fooled by appearances. I pondered this idea, but someone else recognized him, and he became engaged in another conversation. I walked over to speak with Nora before I left. She was in a conversation with Gordon. She turned and spoke to me. "Thank you for coming," Nora said softly, "Steve never spoke of you."

"We were college buddies. We both attended San Jose State University. It was cheap and crowded, and I suppose his father would have wanted him at Stanford or Berkeley, but I don't think Steve had the grades. We had some classes together, but I wasn't a member of his fraternity. I saw him only rarely after we graduated," I said.

"Gordon tells me Steve asked you to stay at the cabin. Did you enjoy reminiscing?" she asked.

"Somewhat, but I was hoping to talk about doing some business with him, but we never had the chance."

"Oh," Nora said and looked down as if I failed her questioning.

When she looked up, a sweet smile crossed her face, and Nora turned her attention elsewhere. I was both relieved and deflated. It was a curious mixture, but as the room was becoming claustrophobic, it was time to leave. A few guests left with me, while others were still arriving at the door.

Beth was near the front door standing with her husband, and I wanted to say goodbye. I wanted to be polite, but I couldn't tell her how great she looked, or how the years had treated her kindly. They hadn't. I hoped I would think of something to say.

"I would have rather seen you again after all these years under better circumstances. I'm glad that you remember me," I commented.

"I understand you were at the cabin when it happened," Beth stated flatly.

I was annoyed by her abruptness. "Yes, I was at the cabin, but Steve didn't die at the cabin. I wasn't there when he died," I said.

I looked at Beth's husband for support, but he only walked away toward other guests. Beth had not even introduced him properly to me.

"I suppose you remember Steve and me as a couple in college, but we broke up shortly after graduation. I ran into him years later, and we built up a close friendship. At times, I cared about Steve more than my husband Jim thought appropriate. Steve knew that and even became a patient of my husband, who is a dentist here in Marin. They became friends as well. We often had dinner at their house, but Nora and I never became close," Beth admitted.

"When did Steve inherit his father's business?" I asked.

"A few years ago, shortly after his father's death, only a year after Steve lost his mother to cancer. It was difficult for Steve to lose them both over so short a period. Steve's father liked Nora, but his mother never approved of her."

"You may be somewhat harsh on Nora." I said.

Beth looked at me as if we were strangers, which we really were.

"Be careful," she said. "Nora is a determined person. She gets what she wants."

"So warned," I mused.

I gladly retreated shortly after that.

## *Ten*

Some months later, I was eating lunch at a busy restaurant in San Francisco when I was approached by a man about my age.

"Okay," he said. "I gained some weight and lost some hair since college. Still, I thought you would recognize me."

After I looked closer at the man, I did recognize him. "I didn't know you worked in the city," I said.

"I don't work in San Francisco," he said. "Business trip. When I come here, I sometimes would visit Steve at his office in Marin. We even did some business together. Old college buddies need to stick together, don't you think?" he said as he slapped me on the back. "I heard about his death. Strange circumstances, huh?"

"Somewhat strange," I replied, thinking more about his remark about their doing business together. Not noticing my squirming, he continued with what he wanted to say.

"We would talk about his cabin occasionally. After his father died, Steve didn't visit the cabin as much. His wife, Nora, really didn't like to go up there. Steve was the one who enjoyed fishing at the lake. That's what seems so odd," he said.

"What seems odd?" I said impatiently.

"Don't you remember?" he said. "Steve never learned to swim. His father brought the whole family from the Midwest when Steve was just a kid. His father who grew up in the Midwest, never thought it important to learn. We used to tease Steve. He could barely float without a life jacket. He always wore one when fishing. That is why I was surprised to learn he had drowned, and even more surprised when they said he might have committed suicide. If that were true, I doubt he would have chosen drowning."

There was no life jacket at the scene, I said to myself.

"I just talked with him the week before," the man continued.

"How did he seem to you?" I asked.

"Steve said he and his wife were spending lots of money, and then laughed. He seemed upbeat."

I changed the topic, and we parted shortly after, but my puzzlement wouldn't go away. I recalled the image of Steve's body caught in the spillway. He wasn't wearing a life jacket and there wasn't one nearby. Furthermore, there was no mention of the boat I had seen at the dock. Why would he go out in the lake alone?

For the remainder of the day, I remained puzzled by his comments. I decided to follow up by contacting Sheriff Thompson at his office.

"Hello Julie," I said. "This is Matthew Handley. Do you remember me from my visit?"

"Sure do. That was a very stressful time for us all. Did you want to talk to Frank? I will transfer you to him."

Then Frank got on the line. I was sure he wasn't as busy as when I was there. I told him what I had learned about Steve not knowing how to swim.

"I didn't realize that. At the lake, he never let on, even as a teenager. But then again, I never saw him swimming, but he did love fishing and he always wore a life jacket and others did tease him about it," Frank said.

"Was there any question about the cause of death?" I asked.

"Well, it was drowning, of course. But we did discover that before Steve came to the cabin, he withdrew all his money from the bank.

There is an insurance investigator nosing around here because, if it was an accident, they pay off his insurance—not so with a suicide. What is your opinion?" Frank asked.

"I don't know. Today I ran into a friend of his who told me Steve didn't know how to swim and always wore a lifejacket. I recalled that Steve wasn't found wearing one. But then again, I didn't know Steve was on the lake in a boat. Was he?" I asked. "I was hoping you had the answers."

All I heard was a sigh on the end of the line. "No additional answers yet. I will call you if we find any," said Frank.

I felt relieved giving my responsibility for all my concerns and questions over to Frank and hung up the phone without any more thoughts to the questions I raised.

The next few days were busy at the office, and I didn't have time or energy to spend on anything other than lots of phone calls to possible leads for clients, and paperwork for the few clients I did have. As a matter of fact, I was deeply involved with a new client's complicated portfolio when Sheriff Thompson called on my cell phone.

"The insurance investigator has raised a lot of questions and the story never settled well with me either," Frank said. "I hoped Steve was running away from his problems and had an unfortunate accident near the dam on the way to the parking area near the old hotel. And that's why he had taken his money from the bank. I can't believe it was a suicide because of that. It just doesn't seem plausible. I am sure Steve would make a different choice. I believe that, and so does the investigator."

"The insurance investigator doesn't think it was suicide?" I asked.

"Well, he hopes it was a suicide as there was a sizable policy on Steve."

"How much is the policy for?" I asked.

"One million," Frank said, "But the investigator says that amount is not unusual for a business owner. However, he needs the issue cleared up, since the cause of death has not been determined. I have received nasty calls from everyone involved, including Nora, her lawyer, Steve's partner, and even Beth."

"I guess we really stirred the pot," I said.

"I can't blame them for being upset. They want it over with," Frank said.

# *Eleven*

Beth called me at home that same day. Annoyed, I didn't ask how she obtained my phone number.

"I am angry," Beth shouted into the phone. "Nora couldn't even wait a year! She has put the cabin on the market. She wants to sell it right away. Steve's father wanted the cabin to stay in the family."

"From what I have heard, Nora may need the money," I said in her defense.

"Not really. Nora does all right. She is anxious to settle with the insurance company, however."

"I am right in the middle of writing a contract, so I have to go," I said. "I need to finish up this paperwork at home before I leave. Skiing is supposed to be good this weekend at Dodge Ridge, and I plan to take advantage and spend the weekend in the mountains."

"Good for you. Maybe you could stop by and check with Sheriff Thompson on the way. See if he knows anything new," she said.

"Maybe Beth, but don't count on it," I replied and ended the conversation. I have no intention of spoiling my time away. I have been looking forward to this trip.

At my apartment about an hour later, my cell phone rang again as I was about finished packing. Grumbling about the number of phone calls received that day, I reluctantly picked it up. Usually I let calls at home go to my voicemail, but there is something about consistent ringing that just makes me pick it up. The caller was Nora.

"You sound rushed. Is this a bad time to call?" she asked.

"I am just packing for a weekend ski trip," I replied.

"I heard you were going to the mountains for skiing," she said.

Beth had obviously been busy on the phone.

"As you already know, the cabin is for sale. If you want, I could tell the realty company to give you a key and you could stay there," she said.

"Thanks, but no, the memories of that cabin aren't really terrific for me," I said.

"I understand, but in case you should change your mind, I will give them a call anyway. Call me when you get back. I have some ideas how we could work together."

I was surprised by the comment. I suppose I could have asked her, but I didn't know how to respond.

"Bye for now," Nora said and hung up. It seemed she was always the one in charge.

I thought to myself, how strange that a friend I hadn't seen in many years was now such a part of my life.

~ * ~

Skiing was the best it had been in recent years in the Sierras and early. I had decided to try out the small ski area, Dodge Ridge, which Kit at the Sugar Pine Inn had recommended. The previous year had been a blowout, he said. The snowfall didn't come until late and only real diehards went in early spring.

This year, however, the snowfall was early and set up for a good ski season. Many times in the last few years, my friends and I would start out thinking we would have an amazing time and were disappointed in either a change in the weather, or a bad experience in trying to drive to the ski resort. In the few times everything seemed perfect, everyone in the Bay Area was on the road for the same reason and traffic was unbearable.

But this time, for whatever reason, everything was perfect. There was not much traffic, the sky was filled with sunshine, and the snow pack was perfect...not too powdery, just right for easy skiing. By Sunday afternoon, I was pleasantly tired and ready to return home. I was alone in my car.

The weather continued to remain fair, and as I approached Sugar Pine, I saw the turnoff. In an instant decision, I swerved the car into the turnoff lane and followed my instincts into the town. It was easy to find the realty company as it was the only one. The realtor seemed eager to sell me the cabin, but I explained I was a friend of Nora and just wanted to look at it before I left the mountains and, if I didn't hurry, I wouldn't be able to look at all. Reluctantly, she gave me the key, hoping for a sale. She waved eagerly from the front door of her office. I could see her figure dimming in the distance as I careened down the mountain highway heading off for the cabin. It wasn't long before I reached the familiar circular driveway.

I wandered through the cabin and ended up in the bedroom where I had stayed the previous time. I remembered barging into a quarrel when I first came to the cabin and the subsequent friendliness between the two men the remainder of the evening until the second quarrel outside my bedroom door. Then, there was my journey around the lake looking for Steve and seeing nothing over the dam spillway until the next day when the searchers discovered his body. I didn't find anything unusual in the cabin and decided to take a look outside.

I walked down the path to the clearing where I had stopped before and looked back at the cabin while I sat on a large rock. I thought I spotted someone standing at the cabin door, but when I blinked and looked again, the figure had vanished. My imagination was getting the better of me, and it was probably the shadow from the tree limb of a large pine tree.

# Twelve

The tree was surrounded by stones obviously brought up from the lake for that purpose. The area nearby appeared to have been cleared in earlier times, but now only pine needles were covering it. I stopped to rest a second. Sitting on the boulder, I noticed lots of ants crawling around, and I squirmed to get them off me. I noticed the initials S + B carved into the rock. Did the initials stand for Steve and Beth? What puzzled me were the marks were recently made, not twenty or so years ago. Looking around the boulder, I discovered a large, leveled worn spot, possibly someone or some animal had rested there. Maybe the boat had rested there, and that idea gave me the impetus to check out the storage shed where the boat might have been taken since no one was using the cabin.

The shed door was locked, but after fumbling around with the keys the realtor had provided, I found the correct one and opened it. Inside, I found the motorboat, wooden and old, but it sported a shiny new motor, a half-filled gas can, paddles for an emergency and, of course, life jackets.

Suddenly I heard the shed door slam and darkness enveloped me. I yelled out of instinct and, just as suddenly, the door opened. There stood a wiry old man with faded clothes and an old hat covering his wrinkled face which looked displeased.

"What are you doing here?" he asked. "My name is Tom Sanders, and I live next door. I was walking around and saw the shed door was open and thought someone had forgotten to close it. Why were you sneaking around?"

"I was not sneaking around," I stammered. "I got the keys from the realtor. See?"

"Damn realtors. Damn sellers. Shouldn't be selling these cabins. Steve should know better," Tom said.

"Well, your next-door neighbor Steve is dead," I stated brusquely.

"I know that!" Tom shouted. "Well then, his relatives should know better. Don't like all these people wandering around here. Nuisance, that's what it is."

"Who else has been around?" I asked.

"Lots of people. Realtors, buyers, nosy people, and, of course, the investigator," Tom said.

"Have you talked with the investigator?" I asked.

"Sure—had to—he kept coming around until I did."

"What did you tell him?" I asked.

"Why should I tell you?"

"I was here when Steve died. I was a friend of his. It bothers me that they still don't seem to know what happened," I said.

"Well, I don't want to get involved," he said. "But I know what happened."

"You do?"

"Sure. That night I couldn't sleep. It has been happening more and more as I get older. So I sat on my back porch and looked at the lake in the full moon. I saw someone quietly motor back to the dock. Very unusual. I waited and the person walked back to the cabin. It looked like Steve in his red plaid shirt, but then again it was dark, and I didn't have my glasses on."

"Did you tell this to the investigator," I asked.

"He didn't ask me. Shouldn't have told you," he said, and with that comment he turned to start heading back to his cabin.

"What time was it?" I asked, calling after him.

"Around midnight," Tom said.

"Are you sure?" I asked."

"Damn sure. I looked at my watch. It was around midnight, and he was walking back from the dock. I may be old, but I'm not stupid," Tom yelled back.

That's odd. Is the old man just mistaken about who he saw and when?

I had a lot on my mind. I walked back up to Steve's cabin, and settled on one of the chairs in the kitchen thinking about what the old man had said. I stared at the land phone on the small table near the refrigerator. I hadn't noticed the answering machine next to it when I was staying as a guest. I didn't recall Frank discovering it either.

The answering machine was old and inexpensive. The calls were preserved in its memory, so I pressed the play button and listened to the unanswered calls. There were two of them.

The first caller was a woman. I recognized the voice as Beth. She said, "Steve, I apologize for getting carried away the other night. I even told my husband about the initials and was surprised he wasn't angry. Thanks for understanding." Her voice seemed soft and apologetic.

The second caller was Nora. She sounded as if she were trying to bolster Steve. "Take care, my darling. After this weekend, everything is going to work out. Have faith in our plans," she said.

I opened the small drawer under the table top hoping to find an address book. What I found instead was a cluster of photos of the four friends in various poses in and out of the cabin. There was a matchbook in the drawer as well. I took two of the photos and the matchbox and decided to visit Sheriff Thompson instead of calling. He had given me his home address, and his house seemed to be located near the realty company where I could return the keys in an outside drop.

I locked the cabin door and stuffed the keys in my pocket along with the photos and the matchbook. Driving to the sheriff's house was easy, but I didn't know if he would appreciate my dropping in on him on his day off. I found him at home and, oddly enough, the sheriff seemed pleased to see me.

"Welcome," Frank said and smiled from inside his screen door.

Frank's house was located on the outskirts of the small town, on a comfortable side street with few other houses for company. It was an old house, in a style from the past, with a shaded porch, and a few old rose bushes framing the wooden structure. Painted white, it blended with the proverbial picket fence from the same era. The whole scene was like a photo tourists take in these old towns. I wondered if he lived here alone. As if he heard my question, Frank answered.

"I moved back here to my childhood town after my wife left me and my daughter. The big city was never what I wanted, and so I returned. My daughter was only three years old at the time. But she never really liked it here, especially when she became a teenager. Too small for her so she moved in with my sister in Seattle and got married there later. She wants me to move to Seattle when I retire. No chance of that. I like it here," Frank said.

"Well, I'm sorry I disturbed your Sunday at home. I also appreciate your not thinking me a fool," I said.

Frank offered me tea. My picture of him in his cowboy hat and boots didn't line up with him drinking tea on a weekend. I declined, but I must have looked surprised by his offer.

Frank explained when he brought himself the iced tea.

"Don't drink anymore. I once had a problem with alcohol," the sheriff said. "You are wondering about these odds and ends you have discovered and so am I. Or perhaps we are both just curious people. What is it now?"

I told him of my visit to the cabin, the messages on the tape recorder, the talk with the old man, and the discoveries in the shed.

He wrinkled his face while he listened.

"Well, the messages seem harmless, but I wonder about the neighbor's recollection. I don't like loose ends and inconsistencies. It seems the matter won't settle down. I have been pondering about some things myself," he said.

I moved forward in my chair to listen closely.

"None of what I found out is really important either, just confusing. On the very morning before you arrived, it seems Steve came into town, stopped at the gas station, saw the mechanic, bought some groceries, and came to visit me. When I talked to him, and when the others chatted with him, Steve did not seem despondent or distraught. He almost made a point of being seen around this little town and being remembered as being happy. He acted, and this is just my opinion, like a man about to run away and have people remember that day as a normal one."

"That is especially suspicious since that evening Steve made a point of going out to get our dinner in the village," I said.

"That does line up with his making a point of people noticing him in town. Well, with the investigator nosing around, more ideas should turn up. The investigator wants it to be a suicide, so his company won't have to pay, but it is not looking that way. It could have been such a bad decision on Steve's part and an accident."

"Maybe both of us should sleep on our suspicions and ideas, and call each other later," I proposed.

"Sounds good," Frank said."

I returned the key to the realtor and left town. I returned to the city in darkness and enjoyed a late supper before returning to my apartment. I went right to bed, exhausted both physically and mentally from the weekend. Enjoying the comfort and security of my own place, I fell asleep quickly. It was morning when I realized I had neglected to show the sheriff the photos and the matchbook.

# *Thirteen*

I walked slowly to work on Monday morning. No one drives a car in the city, and I usually take a bus, but I wasn't quite ready for work after such a busy weekend. Besides, it was a gorgeously sunny day, especially for San Francisco. Tourists always complain about the fog in the warm months. Even the locals get tired of it. Nobody appreciates beautiful sunny days more than San Franciscans. The sun shines through the tall skyscrapers pointing to a cloudless, blue sky like a beam in a forest of concrete. Such a day always raises my spirits.

Several clients called that morning, and it looked like a great start to a productive week at work. I needed an infusion of new clients and many prospective clients even returned my messages, but I wasn't prepared for one of the calls. It was Nora.

"Well, are you interested in buying my cabin?" she asked with a giggle in her voice.

"Not really. I just thought I might suggest it to a friend," I lied.

"I'm glad you are really not a potential buyer, "Nora said. "It would muddy our relationship. I'm considering hiring you as my personal financial consultant though. Could we have lunch together and discuss the possibility?"

I couldn't think of any plausible or moral reason not to take her as a client. Nevertheless, my instincts told me it was probably not a good idea, but I would be curious to learn more about her finances. It meant sparring with her, and she seemed a formidable opponent.

"Were you thinking of today?" I asked. "You could come to my office so I can show you around, and then I could take you to lunch," reasoning I could write it off as a business expense.

"Today is fine. I look forward to seeing you again," Nora said and hung up.

I couldn't shrug off the feeling of being seduced, which was rare but exciting. I couldn't help being flattered by her attention as she was a stunning woman.

When she arrived precisely at twelve o'clock, I wasn't surprised. But I was always amazed when people carried out that feat. I usually arrived late except when I made a special effort as with business appointments. Never at the exact moment.

In the office were the receptionist, a young woman in her early twenties, two aging unmarried brothers who were clients of an associate, and a teenage boy impatiently waiting for his mother to finish her business in another room. All noticed Nora's entrance. It wasn't so much what Nora was wearing, although her outfit was well-fitted and tasteful, but it was more the presence she brought to the setting. Nora strolled into the room as an actress walks across a stage, demanding your attention.

Long ago, when I first moved into my office, I arranged my desk in front of the window so I could view prospective clients as they entered. I always thought this gave me an advantage. I knew beforehand much about their attitude and mood before officially seeing them. Today, I had a box seat for Nora's entrance. I came out of my office to welcome her, and all those people in the reception room looked at me as Nora entered my office. I felt special, too.

"It's nice to see you again under more pleasant circumstances," Nora said and sat in the chair in front of my desk.

"I hope you will like some ideas I have," I replied.

"I'm eager to hear them," Nora said. "With Steve's death, I became a full partner in his business. With his assets, I also inherited his debts, of which there are many. Fortunately, Steve was insured, so the settlement should cover our debts. I am looking for a financial consultant for my personal investments, not, as you may suppose, to rescue me from debt."

"And I'm assuming that includes reinvesting the money Steve withdrew from your joint checking and saving accounts before he died?" I asked.

Nora could barely hide her surprise. "When I learned of the withdrawals, I immediately replaced them, for the time being at least."

"Why do you suppose he made those withdrawals?" I asked.

"I have no idea, but I suppose many thoughts were occurring to him. Perhaps running away was one of them," Nora offered.

"Sheriff Thompson has made the same assumption," I suggested.

"I see you have done some research," Nora said.

"Does that bother you?"

"Not necessarily. As a matter of fact, I am impressed at your being so thorough."

"Well, then, let's continue our discussion during lunch. I have some ideas for your investments, but I do need a little more information."

As we left my office, the receptionist's eyes trailed us. The patrons and staff at the restaurant noticed us too. Nora is such a striking figure. She demands attention and is well aware of her impact on people, I thought. I believe Nora is why we were seated at such a good table.

During lunch, I surmised why Nora was so good at the art of conversation. Part of her charm emanated from her unending supply of bits and pieces of information about current affairs. She wove her knowledge of travel and finances into her remarks. I could see how effective Nora would have been as Steve's partner at social events.

Instead of just spending his money, Nora must have been an asset to his business as well. It was obvious she enjoyed being the center of conversation, and I could not picture her being any other way. The hour lunch lengthened into two and finally I returned to work without her. I believed the receptionist was disappointed at my solo entrance. She was as entranced as I was by Nora.

# *Fourteen*

At home that evening, I gathered the photos and the matchbook and studied them at the kitchen table. The name of a restaurant was the background in one of the photos and the same name and logo was featured on the book of matches. I decided I would have lunch there the next day.

The upscale restaurant was located near the Embarcadero at the street level of a newer building almost completely enshrouded in glass. The name was boldly draped across the front of the building in old barnwood lettering. Quite trendy. There was absolutely no parking available, but I had taken a taxi. When I entered, I passed the maître d's front desk where the menus where framed behind the desk on the wall illuminated by a discreet lamp. I knew I wouldn't like the prices, but I was certain I would like the entrees.

I didn't know what information I expected to garner, but I was certainly going to try. Armed with the photos I had taken on my amateur sleuthing day, I first informed the maître d of my reservation which was a half hour later. I told him my date would be arriving then, but in truth, I hadn't invited anyone. I was going to make up some excuse for not using the reservation.

I made my way into the small bar for a drink. Even the drink was expensive, but the bartender certainly made it worthwhile. Dressed in a no-nonsense but well-tailored black suit, the lady bartender wore her blonde hair tied back in a bun. She wore long, trailing silver earrings that framed her face. I was charmed before she ever spoke to me, and, thankfully, her voice was as impressive as her slim black uniform. I had to remind myself I was on a serious mission. Maybe I could come back next week for a drink.

"What will you have, sir?" she asked.

"Dirty martini," I said, and refrained from making a bad joke.

"Good choice. I make an excellent one," she replied.

When she returned with my drink, I tried to gaze as if I were interested, which I really wasn't faking, and she lingered.

"Are you here by yourself?" she asked.

"For now. I am meeting some friends," I lied. She smiled as if to imply that made more sense than my being alone. I really liked her.

"They don't seem to be here yet. You didn't see them earlier, did you? Maybe I mixed up the time."

She fell for my line, and I showed her the photos.

"Not all of them are coming, of course. But two of them are supposed to meet me here."

"Sure," she said. "I recognize the friends you are expecting. They seem to be such a nice couple."

I pointed to one couple, Beth and her husband. She shook her head and pointed to another person.

"Well, they aren't standing next to each other in the photo, but they are usually very cozy and seeming to be in love when they are here." She pointed to Nora and Beth's husband, Jim.

I was surprised but tried not to show it.

"I haven't seen them in a few days, however," she said before she was called away by another customer at the bar.

I lingered at the bar with my thoughts and my dirty martini. When I finished my drink, I returned to tell the maître d that my girlfriend had called and said she wasn't coming. He was not happy with this news, but he caught himself and expressed that he hoped to see us back soon.

I left and walked some distance before hailing a taxi. I was trying to decide if I would say anything of what I had found to either Nora or Sheriff Thompson. I had told no one of my discovery of the photos, or my intended visit to the restaurant. At least for now, keeping it to myself seemed the best option.

# *Fifteen*

When I got back to my office, I checked my e-mails and found an invitation to a party at Nora's house. She added a note saying one of Steve's closest friends had missed the reception for Steve, and after the service had e-mailed her and suggested another gathering of Steve's old friends. This time, he hinted, it would be like what Steve would have enjoyed. It would be a wake in his honor with old tunes and long-lost friends only. Nora said at first she was hesitant, but the longer Steve's friend talked about doing it, the more convincing was the idea. A lot of his old college friends would be there, and Nora wanted me to accept her invitation.

She said there would be lots of drinks and food, as well as a live band playing music from that era. Even though I was hesitant to attend, I thought possibly I could make some new business contacts... even though I realized most of the guests probably already had financial consultants. Anyway, I considered myself out of their league. But when I called, Nora assured me she would introduce me around and relate how she used my services for her personal finances.

The usual suspects were there, Beth and her good-looking dentist husband, Jim, and Gordon, who I really didn't want to see again. Of course, as I rang the doorbell and the door was opened by the maid and I walked in, they were the first guests standing in the foyer in full view. I hoped that among all the many guests invited I could just blend in and possibly avoid them altogether, but that was not to be. Thankfully, Nora appeared out of nowhere, always the gracious hostess, and eased the greetings among us, especially between Gordon and me.

"Glad you decided to come," she said. "There are lots of good prospects here, and I will be sure to introduce you to them."

At that remark, Gordon grimaced. Beth replied with her usual sarcasm. "How are you?" she asked. "Still snooping around?"

"I believe I am finished with that," I replied, truly believing I was finished with any involvement in this mess. I was irked by her comment, nevertheless.

"Well," said her husband, Jim, "all this business about Steve was disarming, but we all hope the insurance company settles soon."

Yeah, I thought to myself, and money for more parties that Steve will pay for and can't attend. How nice.

"Think I will mingle," I said, hoping to get away from this intimate circle.

Before I left this charming small group, Gordon mumbled, "Steve would have wanted things to quiet down after his accident."

"Yeah," I said sarcastically while turning away, "Steve was the quiet one."

I wandered off to one of the outside patios with a sweeping view of the San Francisco Bay and listened to the music. Nora had hired a group of musicians to play music from our college days as a tribute to happier times. The musicians looked uncomfortable in formal attire with their long hair tied up in ponytails and wisps of tattoos sneaking out here and there. They did their best to look enthusiastic about the old tunes and did a good job of reviving them. As the songs continued, I reminisced about those college days when Steve and I were dancing and drinking, well at least he was dancing whereas I was mostly drinking. Steve had much more success with the ladies than I.

Steve was the gregarious one. Entering a party in progress, he played the role he loved. When someone answered the doorbell and swung open the door, Steve would always step back, as if surprised, and then enter the room and survey. Like a politician entering a crowded event, Steve would high-five every guy, look him straight in the eye and say something personal.

For a woman, he would step back and pronounce some kind of admiration for the way she looked. He had that rare ability only the rest of us could observe; making each person feel special as if he were sincerely interested. He worked the room as if he needed each vote to win a popularity contest, and it worked. He was the center of attention at every party I ever attended with him.

One time after a party at which I observed him charm the guests, I commented about his ability and he just laughed.

"I learned that trick watching my dad," he said. "But my dad really loved people and was sincere in his remarks. On the other hand, I just use it to win people over. It's kind of funny how easy it is."

I was shocked by his confession and asked if he used this trick on me.

"No," he replied. "You are so honest and straightforward it would be more difficult, and besides, I really like you for those qualities. But you should watch out, someone could easily fool you."

I never forgot his warning from that night because I knew he was right. I tried not to be so gullible. Although I tried not to be taken in over the years, I caught myself believing in people who didn't deserve it.

In college, Steve also drove an eye-catching bright colored convertible that attracted women. The ladies clustered around him on and off the road, but he was involved with Beth for most of the time. If I had gone to a party and one of them was with someone else, I would have been surprised.

## *Sixteen*

Beth, at that time, was fun-loving and vivacious. Her long, blonde hair flowed down her back like the stereotype of a cheerleader, which she was at the time. She was as aware of her attractiveness as was Steve and was as free spirited as he; his complete mirror image in many ways. She majored in who-knows-what but managed to graduate in something. The Beth of today was totally different, and I still had a hard time accepting the difference. Just as I was thinking of this, she appeared at my side as if on cue. With a drink in her hand and slurring her words, it was evident she was feeling better than usual.

"Enjoying the music?" she asked, resting her hand on my shoulder.

Her whole countenance had changed since college days. Even though the years hadn't been kind, she threw back her blonde hair as if they had been and smiled broadly.

"Nora does throw a good party," she said. "Good house for it."

She put down her glass on a nearby patio table and sat down, indicating I should join her, which I did.

"Steve and I would have had parties like this all the time," she remarked. "Sometimes I wonder what life would be like for me today if we had married."

Her drinking allowed her to open up to me. I realized she had struggled to hold back her feelings for Steve all these years. I was probably the only person at this party she could talk to about this, so I listened.

"Nora is probably what he really wanted," Beth said. "Steve didn't want to have children, but I did. He wanted the parties to continue after college. I think Steve needed them, but I wanted to settle down and have a family, a house, you know, suburbia and all that. Not Steve. We fought like crazy until we finally broke up. Steve's first wife was a sweet lady and put up with his adolescent longings and his reluctance to have children. She must have agreed not to have a family, but it was rumored she did want one. After she passed away, Steve met his match in Nora. She liked to party as much as he did, and Nora spent even more money than him."

"And you never liked Nora? Why?" I asked.

"Not really. I put up with her because I wanted to see Steve. The four of us would have dinner together and occasionally travel together for a few days, but no, I really don't like her much. Too brassy for me," Beth said, sipping at her drink.

"All in all, you seem to have done quite well, Beth," I said, knowing that a dentist in Marin probably made more money than I.

"Well, our house isn't quite as extravagant as Nora and Steve's house, and it has no view but is closer to the schools. Our children are growing up and I am beginning to have more time for myself. I do miss the excitement and flair Steve generated," Beth said, staring down at her almost finished drink.

I knew what Beth meant. Even if it wasn't sincere at times, Steve's banter always cheered you up and he had a way of making an ordinary event special. Sometimes, years later, I would remember something we did together, when some incident or remark would remind me of him.

"My life is not very exciting," I said.

She looked at me closely.

"Well," Beth said, "You are single and living in San Francisco. It could be."

"Yes, but I don't make much money, I am divorced with no kids, and I haven't really had a relationship with a woman since the divorce."

"Oh," Beth replied. "Really?"

So she changed the subject and we chatted about the view of the bay and made a half-hearted commitment to have lunch together sometime soon. Finally, Beth got up and walked a little awkwardly to the sliding glass door to go inside and probably get another drink. I remained, hoping to work up my courage to return inside when I spotted an attractive red-haired woman about my age talking to Nora. Maybe I would get lucky today. Instead of a new client, maybe Nora could introduce me to a lonely beautiful lady instead.

I walked over to Nora just as the redhead was leaving her. Then I changed my mind. Beth had managed to bring my spirits down a notch and trying to be smart and funny with a new woman seemed too difficult at the moment. Nora still hadn't introduced me to anyone as a good business contact.

So for the last moments of the party before I finally left, I collected four business cards and gave away five of mine. That seemed good work for one day. I left when the music was still playing and drove back to the city. Maybe I would call Beth and take her to lunch. Could I be still interested in their melodrama?

# Seventeen

After I drew up my proposals, my next appointment with Nora came one week later. It was scheduled for four o'clock, and as I had little work lined up for the afternoon that Friday, I decided to call Beth and invite her to lunch as we had talked about at the party. It was last minute, but I decided to give it a chance. She answered on the second ring, but not graciously.

"Oh, it's you," she said. "I was expecting another call."

"I won't keep you," I replied. "I want to invite you to lunch as promised. Can you make it today?" I asked.

Beth stammered something about errands and kids, but finally agreed to my invitation. We agreed to meet at noon at a small restaurant not far from my office.

When I arrived, I found her already seated at a table. She looked the same as when I had last seen her, with even less makeup and a hurried appearance. Even though I was only a few minutes late, she looked annoyed and impatient. I tried to recall the image of her in college, late most of the time and always ready to party with friends.

It was a long time ago. I had barely been seated before Beth started quizzing me.

"I understand you have seen a lot of Nora lately. You two are getting to know each other well," she stated flatly.

"We're doing some business together. We're finishing up today, as a matter of fact," I replied.

She raised her eyebrows but said nothing.

"I understand you and Sheriff Thompson have, too," Beth related. "Did he mention he was the one who introduced Nora to Steve?"

I shook my head. I was surprised by this comment.

Even if I hadn't wanted to hear it, Beth began telling me the whole story.

"After we graduated from college and broke up, Steve spent the next two summers at the cabin, helping his dad with repairs and such. Steve lived at the cabin those two summers while his dad only came up on occasional weekends. Steve invited old college friends to the cabin."

The waiter came by, and Beth ordered a glass of wine. She obviously wasn't ordering lunch yet, and she had a lot to say. I declined and just ordered a glass of water.

"During the second summer," Beth continued, "Nora moved into town with her father, who had found a job as a mechanic at the local gas station. She tried to fit in with the local crowd whose parents had cabins at the lake but wasn't successful. She was dating Frank, who is now the sheriff and lives there year-round."

Beth was obviously enjoying telling her story. "One night when Steve was hanging out at the bar with his friends, Frank introduced Nora to Steve, and according to the guys, that night Nora went full throttle to get Steve interested in her. She and Steve began seeing each other after that summer. Steve's father offered her a job in the city with one of his subcontractors, and they were married a year after that," Beth said.

"How do you know all these details?" I asked.

"The four of us have spent a lot of time together these last few years. I heard the story many times from Steve, but Nora never liked him telling it. She seemed embarrassed by it."

Beth had ordered a glass of wine before I arrived, and when the waitress came with her second one, I encouraged her to order food. Originally, I was hoping for a quick lunch and back to the office, but now I found myself hoping lunch would last longer. I was curious about her perspective of these events.

"I do hope your business with Nora ends today. She likes to keep people involved with her," Beth said. "You may think I'm jealous and that I wished I had married Steve instead of her. That may be true, but Nora has a way of involving people in her life, and it isn't always pleasant."

"Do you wish you had married Steve?" I asked, hoping Beth would not get angry.

"That's not the point," Beth bellowed, showing the effects of her drinking.

"When I was at the cabin I found fresh marks on a rock near the cabin's dock with your initials," I said, not believing I'd said it. I thought she might spray her wine in my face or slam back her chair and walk away, but Beth did neither of those things. Instead, she just stared at me for a few moments before replying.

"I don't have to explain, but I will," Beth began. "It happened one night when the four of us were at the cabin. Steve and I got drunk and silly, and we wandered off into the back yard and carved our initials into the rock. We were drunk, and it was a foolish prank, nothing more. Later, I apologized to Steve for getting so drunk. He just laughed about the incident. Even my husband, when I told him about it, laughed and was not angry."

"Sorry for my rudeness and being so personal after all these years. I was just curious. And thanks for the warning, but you needn't worry. Our business concludes today. Besides, whoever said I was attracted to Nora?"

"Everyone," Beth quipped.

"And just who is everyone?" I asked.

"Just our little group, and possibly Frank," Beth answered. "You do know that Nora was probably having an affair with someone at the time of Steve's death?"

However, as we had nothing else to talk about, we both let that comment slide and we finished lunch without any more personal exchanges. The silence was overwhelming.

## *Eighteen*

After lunch, I returned to the office. When I arrived, the receptionist said a gentleman was waiting for me. I didn't have any appointments except the one with Nora, so I was surprised to see Gordon waiting. He looked angry.

"Step into my office," I invited.

"I suppose you are wondering why I am here," he threw at me before I could say another word. "I am disturbed by your interference in my business affairs. I don't appreciate your interest in what does not concern you." His eyes glittered with anger.

I scowled. "I can assure you I am not trying to interfere in your arrangements," I said. "Nora asked to consult with me on her personal financial matters concerning her upcoming settlement with the insurance company mostly. That's all. I apologize if you feel I have interfered with your business arrangements, but I can assure you I have not."

"Then why have you been snooping around asking a lot of questions about Steve's death? How does his passing affect your business?" Gordon demanded.

"I found myself involved when I was invited to the cabin and Steve disappeared before we had a chance to talk business. I just want to know what happened to him. That's all," I said in my defense.

"It was never my idea to invite you in the first place. It was Steve's idea. As for what happened to Steve. He drowned!" Gordon shouted and banged his fist on my desk.

He was making a scene, and the receptionist, as well as another colleague, were staring through the glass partition. I was fearful my young receptionist might call 911 and I did not want that to happen.

"This is my office and you are making quite a scene. I am asking you to leave," I said calmly.

Gordon slammed his fist down on my desk again. "I'll leave only because I have said what I came here to say. Just stay out of my business and I will stay out of yours!" he shouted in one last parting remark and stormed out. The young receptionist signaled with her hands and mouthed, "Wow!"

I was shaken myself.

Gordon had been a blowhard in his college days and a champion wrestler. I recalled at least one incident in which he had taken a small incident and had blown it into a major problem. Gordon had taken a disliking to the opposing football team...the entire team... and insulted each one from the stands. Gordon did this loudly and security asked him to leave, repeatedly.

After the game, the football players found him at a fraternity party and there was a brawl. This was only one incident in a long list that established Gordon's reputation as a hothead with a bad temper. It seemed he had not mellowed over the years.

~ * ~

Later that day, I was distracted by a phone call from Nora. She sounded upset, but not angry.

"I apologize for Gordon. He told me he was going to pay you a visit. I had hoped to forewarn you, but by the time I got his message and called his office, the receptionist said he had already gone. I am sorry," she said. "I understand Beth has been annoying you, too."

"Not really. We just went out for lunch. You certainly are all wired into each other," I said. "After all, I knew her in college and wanted to see her again."

"Just like Steve," Nora said.

I let that comment slide.

She went on to remark, "I am upset by Gordon's meddling in my affairs and need to talk with him about it. I will assure him that everything is okay and insist he should not be involved in my personal business. Gordon gets overprotective of me sometimes. I will call you to make another appointment, but I can't make it today as I am too upset. Thanks again for all your efforts on my behalf."

I was disappointed Nora would not be coming, but also relieved and decided to leave work early. Before I left, I reviewed again the investments I would be suggesting to her and the tax savings involved. There wasn't a rush to sign anyway as nothing could be finalized until the insurance company paid her claim on Steve's death. Since I wasn't able to help Steve before he died, I found solace in knowing I was helping him inadvertently by helping Nora straighten out her personal finances, separate from the business. She apparently didn't trust the company handling the business finances. She told me that was her reason for asking for my assistance.

I wouldn't want to be involved with Steve's business finances. From what gossip I heard from his friends, I figured either Steve slept through our accounting classes at college, or he just loved spending money. I thought it was probably both prudent and fortunate that I didn't know his financial situation at the end of his life.

I decided that after such an unsettling scene in my office with Gordon, I needed to take a walk and get some fresh air. Walking around the city was always my release from stress and an enjoyable, inexpensive activity. I told the receptionist I probably wouldn't be back later, and she looked relieved that the drama was over for the day.

I grabbed my jacket as the breeze was brisk from the bay and headed toward Chinatown only a few blocks away from the financial district, but a world apart from its type of chaos. One of many walks I had discovered in enjoying the varied neighborhoods of my adopted town was the walk in Chinatown...my favorite. I learned that outside of China, this neighborhood was the largest of its type on the west coast of the United States.

I walked down Bush Street and turned right at Grant Avenue, one of the original streets in the city and a long, and even somewhat sordid, history. As I passed through the gaily decorated dragon gates, the official entrance to Chinatown, I left my cares behind and joined the mix of people jostling down the avenue. This somewhat bizarre mixture of tourists, tour groups, merchants, and every day Chinese buyers and sellers was intoxicating in its variety. I loved the sights and smells of Chinatown. Outside some shops, there were tables of souvenirs of the Golden Gate Bridge, cable cars, tee shirts, and the like mixed in with shops selling jewelry, tea and clothing. No more chickens hanging outside the grocery stores as had been the case in the past, but plenty of dried herbs and spices.

I popped into my favorite bakery that sells small, warm steamed cakes of red bean paste with miniature pieces of barbecued pork hidden inside, called char siu bao. It is my favorite snack, and I nibbled on one while I walked past the tea store with its rows of varied teas selling from a few dollars to hundreds of dollars a pound. Large wooden tables were set up for the tasting. It was part of one of the tours, and I spotted the guide giving the group a short history of San Francisco's Chinatown. I reminded myself how lucky I was to live here.

Walking back through the dragon gates, I reluctantly reentered my world where the problems that had brought me on this walk still existed.

# Nineteen

Nora called me at the office to once again apologize for Gordon's behavior.

"Gordon can be such a bull in a china shop. He doesn't know where to draw the line between protecting me and offending me."

"Well, he certainly can be threatening," I said.

"Let me make it up to you and play tourist guide on a walk on Mt. Tamalpais. It is quite beautiful up there, and I live on the outskirts. We could drive from my house down to the parking lot there and take an easy ocean view trail I know. Lunch could be on me down at Muir Beach. What do you think?"

I felt like she was looking to know me more than just financially, but it wasn't all bad. Even though I had the feeling I was a spider in her web, she was very convincing, and I had always wanted to see the view from Mt. Tam (as the locals call it) and the idea of someone who already knew the trails and lived there was very appealing.

"Okay," I said. "I don't want to talk business."

"No business," Nora repeated.

Why do I have the feeling she will get some information from me nevertheless, but maybe not financial. It is like a con man sizing up his prey and figuring out how the person can be of benefit in his scheme.

"We need to go on a weekday, for weekends are crowded with tourists. Are you available day after tomorrow?" Nora asked.

I would make it available, I said to myself.

"What time shall I come to your house?" I asked her.

"Nine o'clock," she said. "Want to get an early morning start and work up an appetite for lunch after our hike."

I would be happy with bologna and cheese sandwiches, but a restaurant of her choice would probably be more memorable.

"Sounds good. I will bring my appetite along. I'll see you then. Thanks." I ended the call, somewhat nervous about our meeting but also excited about the prospect.

That morning we were to meet, I drove to her house in Marin, nervously anticipating a challenge of wits with a very smart lady. I thought I was ready.

Located across the Golden Gate Bridge, Marin County comes out of the fog and delights the visitor with its proximity to its nearby neighbor, but with its own beach and tall peaks. Mt. Tamalpais rises above the greenery with magnificent views of the city by the bay.

There is a small town called Marin City, but Nora lived in the clouds above the freeway in Mill Valley, a very pricey area. As I drove up to her mansion, I marveled again at its beauty. Set back among trees with its entrance facing the circular driveway, the two-story house had its own separate one-bedroom guesthouse as well as a pool in the back, also draped with more foliage and surrounded by tall trees, giving the house even more privacy.

This time, Nora met me at the door dressed casually for hiking, and we left in her Mercedes down the winding road to the parking lot for Mt. Tamalpais State Park. Nora seemed to know her way around and immediately headed for the easy hike she had chosen, the Ocean View Trail. She knew of a side path off the parking lot called the Old Mine Trail, and so what appeared next was a beautiful vista of the ocean right before us. I was thrilled to be there.

We continued hiking for a while. I am not afraid of heights, but I did stay away from the edge of the path. There were not too many hikers on this weekday, and until Steve's death was cleared up, I would remain cautious. As promised, Nora did not bring up the subject during our hike and I tried hard to relax around her.

"You seem tense," she said at one point.

"No," I replied. "I just am not used to hiking and am concentrating on my steps and the scenery."

"Have you had enough for today? Ready for lunch? Where I am taking you opens at eleven-thirty. It is a local roadhouse very well-known down at Muir Beach, not far from here."

I would love to come back here. But I have had enough hiking for today.

"Sounds good. You make a good trail guide. Did you hike at Sugar Pine a lot while growing up?" I asked her.

"I was under the impression we weren't asking each other questions today," she quipped.

"You are right. Let's go have some lunch. I have worked up an appetite."

We hiked back down to the parking lot and drove on another windy road down to Muir Beach. I was awed that such a sandy, stretched-out beach lay right across from San Francisco. There were many restaurants, but Nora had already made reservations at the roadhouse she had mentioned. It's got to be good, and probably expensive.

I was right on both counts. The menu was extensive and pricey, but we had already agreed she was picking up the tab. I let her make suggestions for us both.

The restaurant had an extensive wine menu, but Nora ordered margaritas with our seared ahi tuna appetizer. As we sipped and appetized away, Nora got my consent on ordering grilled salmon, smoked bacon and avocado sandwiches for both of us. If I ate this way every day, I would be a lot heavier. How did she keep her slim figure?

We kept to our promise, but at the end of lunch, Nora just couldn't help herself.

"I want to ask you one thing. Would that be all right with you?" she asked. "I know we made a promise not to ask questions today."

I geared up my defenses. Here it comes.

"Ask away," I said giving her permission.

"What do you think happened to Steve?"

"That's a big question. Frank and the insurance investigator are the ones you should ask, and they don't even seem to know at this point."

"I am asking you," Nora questioned, staring directly into my face. "I know you have been doing some sleuthing on your own."

Yes, and sleuthing turns out to be very tasking and somewhat dangerous.

I couldn't tell her all that I had learned. It wouldn't be right, since some of it I hadn't even told Frank, or the investigator, and I couldn't reveal any of their information either.

"I am hoping like you that it was an accident so you will get the insurance money, and I do not think he committed suicide. I think he may have been running away from his financial problems and was going to leave for Mexico when he accidentally drowned."

Nora stared hard at me, and I realized I had let something slip.

"Who was he going to Mexico with?" Nora asked.

"I don't know. I thought you might know that."

She drank some water and looked pensive. I really had overstepped the boundary between us and was sorry for my mistake.

"I think we should leave now," she finally responded.

"I'm sorry I upset you," I said.

"It's all right. I am a big girl."

We walked to her car and I knew the day was over. I enjoyed the hike but was sorry I had slipped and revealed more than I should have. She had intended to learn something this day anyway.

# *Twenty*

Exhausted from this recurring drama in which I had involved myself, I wanted to forget about the matter during the weekend, but that didn't happen. Friday evening, Frank called me at home.

"I just had to call. You haven't phoned me in the last couple of days and I was wondering if you had thought of anything else."

Should I just say I no longer want to be involved? Instead, I blurted out what had been on my mind.

"As a matter of fact, I did learn something new," I said, regretting the minute I had opened my mouth. I should just stay out of this. Apparently, I can't help myself.

"What's that?" Frank asked.

"I didn't know you and Steve were more than just fishing partners and that you knew Nora quite well," I blurted out.

"It's no secret around here. Steve and I weren't really friends as kids. He was a weekender—a tourist kid—and I was a local boy. Two different worlds, really. But I did introduce him to Nora, who lived here with her father. Steve kind of stole her from me, but then Nora would never have been happy staying here in this little town. Anyway, it is not important now."

"I guess there is a lot I don't know," I said. "Especially all these alliances. Nora and I were to finish working up her portfolio for her investments with funds she will receive from the insurance settlement. Before our appointment, Gordon paid me quite a visit. He said he was extremely angry at my 'interference,' as he called it. I don't think he appreciates my curiosity. But damn it, I was there the day it happened, and Steve's death keeps bugging me!"

"Well, I choose to ignore your curiosity. You can ask me questions anytime. I am neither sensitive nor extremely busy except for this matter. There is still a lot we are looking into that doesn't seem quite right."

"Like what?" I asked.

"Can't really divulge much about the ongoing investigation, you know. But the insurance claim won't be honored until it is determined whether it was a suicide or an accident, and even if he possibly was running away from his financial problems."

"Are you sure about Steve running away?"

"Not at all. But then nothing seems totally clear right now. All kinds of scenarios are being looked at," Frank said. "Please do call me or come by to visit me if you are here."

"Sure enough, Sheriff," I said, wondering if he really was such a nice guy and more importantly was he still thinking I was involved with this tight group?

I poured myself a tall glass of chardonnay and pondered about what Frank had said. Still not understanding what happened to Steve, I decided to go to bed early, but the amount of char siu bao I had eaten earlier disturbed my rest and I experienced a restless night and a bad dream.

Sometimes when I dream, I force myself to remember the dream's contents the next morning in hopes of understanding its meaning. This is a trick I learned from a psychologist while trying to save my marriage. All those sessions I endured with my ex-wife didn't save our marriage. And this exercise is the only valuable thing I learned. I have used the process many times and it works. Upon awakening in the morning, I concentrate on remembering what I dreamt before it slips away, beginning to end, like the plot of a movie.

That night, I slept restlessly, tossing and turning in a vain attempt, I am sure, to toss off the dream, but it persisted despite my constant movements. No conscious or unconscious effort of mine would deter its course.

I dreamt I was at the cabin in the evening with a full moon illuminating the small lake's surface with twinkling much like miniature lights. In my dream, the lake was visible from the cabin, and from where I stood at the back window I could see all around and across it. No detail was spared. Although the scene was dark except for the moonlight and mysterious from the silence and loneliness it evoked, I watched unafraid as an observer.

I dreamed I stepped outside and noticed directly in front of me the little path leading around the perimeter of the lake. It seemed inviting, so I stepped onto its surface. As I did so, the dream lost much of its ethereal quality, and as the scene grew more real, I became afraid. In a dream, I often try to say to myself, "Wake up, this is not real." Sometimes it works and sometimes it doesn't. This time the dream felt real.

My heart began pounding and my throat went dry. I tried to calm myself with reassuring deep breaths, but I felt totally alone, isolated, and vulnerable. I hate to admit it, I was terrified. I slowly began edging myself around the lake, taking short, slow steps and looking all around me as I walked. Dreading each new step, I decided it would be worse just to stand in one place and wait for something to happen.

Eventually, I came to a clear area...void of pine needles or brush. The view was panoramic, and I paused for a few minutes, taking in the broad image of the still lake. From where I stood, a moving figure appeared below wading into the lake, fully clothed in a shirt and pants. Ankle deep, he was slowly... calmly...wading into the icy water. Only a small wake from his movements trailed the man's journey. I moved closer to the lake, off the path, getting closer to where the man had entered.

Instead of calling out to him, I walked to the very edge of the water, still not touching it. I realized I couldn't go into the lake because there was an invisible boundary not allowing me to trespass into the lake's depths. As I stopped, the man turned and looked over his shoulder at me. He smiled a smile that made me shiver...a maddening smile. The man was Steve, and when I recognized him, he turned around and continued walking deeper into the lake.

It was then I found my voice. I attempted to call out to Steve. It sounded more like the call of a loon, a wailing, turning into a shrill cry when he wouldn't look back. He continued his relentless pace and walked deeper and deeper into the lake as my cries rang out across its surface until the top of his head became submerged and the small wake faded onto the surface. Once again, the surface became smooth. Steve had vanished completely.

Appalled by the scene, I fell silent. I just stood there motionless until I began to hear the sounds of another presence. I heard fast moving steps in the distance, but I couldn't see anything. Finally, as the sounds became louder, I realized they were coming from behind me, and I began to run. My movements seemed slow, suspended in time, and the faster I ran the slower the progress became. My frantic attempts at escape seemed doomed.

Soon my panic shrouded the landscape into darkness, and terrified by my ordeal, I became aware the scene was blending into gray on both sides of my vision, becoming a tunnel. It was if I were running in space and I could no longer hear the footsteps behind me. They too had faded into the continuum and terror engulfed me again, as I awoke with a sudden jerk, my heart racing, grateful for reality but exhausted. I hadn't dreamed so vividly in years, and I wondered what the dream signified. For now, it was enough just to remember its fearful contents.

I decided in its aftermath I needed resolution about Steve's death. I thought about the sheriff who might be holding back information, Steve's friends, who bickered amongst themselves, and the suspicions of the insurance investigator. I contacted him, and he said he could not give me any information because I was not a relative, just a friend.

That left me with only the internet and Nora's personal financial records along with all the little bits and pieces of information I had managed to dredge up.

The following week was my vacation, and I had planned to visit Cabo San Lucas in Baja California with some friends. I wasn't finished with my curiosity, so I decided to take a few days to visit Sugar Pine instead. I would stay at the Sugar Pine Inn as inconspicuously as possible. I wouldn't tell anyone and certainly not the sheriff about my visit. I would try to include the realtor in my conspiracy and be as anonymous as possible. The cabin hadn't been sold, possibly because of the sudden and unresolved death of its owner. I knew my presence probably wouldn't go unnoticed for very long, but I only wanted a day or so, with my computer, in an effort to give it one more try for my peace of mind.

Having made this resolve, I reassured myself of some peaceful dreams to come. With a quick shower and a cup of hot coffee on my way to work, I felt better. I wanted to get as far away as I could from this terrifying dream and the frightening anxiety it had created.

## Twenty-one

This time, I decided to take a less scenic route out of San Francisco to the Sierra Mountains. I drove through Berkeley and Walnut Creek, past Discovery Bay and Stockton, and through the quaint sounding town of Copperopolis. Below Sonora, I joined Highway 108 and traveled on to Sugar Pine.

I decided to visit the cabin when I arrived there, but I didn't know what I expected to find. Maybe I would speak to Frank while there, and then I would head back home. My friends teased me about working too hard as I told them I had to finish some work at my office and would join them later for our vacation. I didn't feel I could reveal to them the real nature of my possible late arrival to Baja.

My one new big account involved Nora, and until the life insurance policy was settled, I wouldn't be paid. That part was true. Maybe if time permitted, I could fly to Cabo and join my friends. Nobody knew I was going to visit Sugar Pine and Steve's cabin. I hadn't told anyone, not even Nora or Frank.

~ * ~

It was early in the week when I drove up. I stopped at the ranger station off Highway 108 near the town of Sugar Pine. The State Ranger, in his full green uniform with his Smoky the Bear hat, was on duty. He greeted me warmly. It was a weekday and off-season so there were few visitors in the station. The interpretative room was adjacent to the information counter and it seems the ranger wanted to use his skills on someone.

"First time here?" he quizzed congenially.

"Yeah," I answered, as I picked up some brochures.

"Where are you headed?"

"Going to stay at Sugar Pine for a day or so."

"This would be really helpful," the ranger said as he picked up a nearby map on a display shelf. "This shows all the features around Sugar Pine and even the road north to Sonora Pass. The road is open now but closed sometimes in the midst of winter."

I headed toward the adjacent interpretative room that was chock full of dusty preserved animal specimens and dried plants behind glass. Mostly I was trying to get away from Smoky, but he followed me.

"So you're staying in Sugar Pine," the ranger repeated. "Quite some history there."

I decided he was a nice enough guy just doing his job and I could at least be polite and listen. The ranger took my silence as a signal he should continue talking.

"The town is named after one of our local pine trees whose cone is the largest of all the pines," and he pointed to a long, slender cone, about eighteen inches long. Indeed it was the largest of all those on display, dwarfing the others. It was the body builder of the pinecones.

"You're right," I commented. "It is quite big."

The ranger beamed broadly at hearing this acknowledgment, and my comments seemed to encourage him to continue.

"You know, then again you might not know, that the Mi-Wuk or Miwok Indians who lived here considered trees as the source of life. They used every part, for food, for baskets in which they carried and cooked their food, for all sorts of things."

"For food?" I asked.

"Well, the Mi-Wuk Indians' main source of food was from acorns from the oak trees, but the pine nuts were staples too, and the pinion, or pine nuts, from the Sugar Pine were prized as the resin is very sweet, hence the pinecone's name. John Muir commented on its sweetness and said the resin was sweeter than maple syrup."

"The Mi-Wuk would collect the sugar pine nuts in the summer. The men would shake some trees climbing very high in order to do this. We have a replica of a Mi-Wuk village over there," he said as he pointed to an adjacent room, "if you would like to look."

"Thanks, but I really should be leaving now."

"Okay." He looked disappointed and then perked up when he remembered something. "You know Sugar Pines' annual Founder's Day Festival is coming up. They will have sugar pine needle tea for you to sample."

"Really?" I commented.

"Don't usually reveal these facts to visitors. Don't want tourists wounding pine trees to get their sap or taking pine needles for tea. Some pines are not wise to try like Yew pine and Norfolk Island pine, and any yew which is really not a pine is dangerous for making tea. There are certain pines whose needles are better than others for such a purpose. Also, the time of year and how long they have been kept, do make a difference. Better to get the tea off the internet, but you can be assured of safety of the tea at Founder's Day."

"Thanks for all your tips," I said, clutching my brochures and map and starting off toward the door. I turned to wave back at him, but the ranger had already found some other tourist to engage in conversation.

I continued on toward Sugar Pine and stopped at the local coffee shop on my way to the realtor's office because I hadn't eaten anything since leaving San Francisco. Coffee shops, especially in small towns, are a great place to eavesdrop on the local gossip, and this place was no exception.

When I pulled into the parking lot, it was early afternoon, and a few old men and one elderly female were still sitting there chatting about politics and local gossip. Just opening the door with the bell jingling at my entrance caused a stir. They all looked up and the waitress rushed to greet me, grateful for a distraction from tidying the napkin holders.

I sat at the counter because as a kid, my grandfather had taken me to a retro 50's style soda fountain, the name given to such restaurants back then. That one had small tables and a counter with a mirror behind it just like this. It had even featured a juke box and photos of that time period. Behind this counter was a waitress with an apron, just like in the movies. I really enjoyed pretending I was a part of a Hollywood set. As she brought me a cup of coffee and what looked like a stale bagel, I asked loudly, "Can you tell me the directions to the realty company?" Of course, I already knew how to get there, but I was trying to cover for my presence in the small town.

"Sure," the waitress said. "What are you looking for? I know all the properties for sale myself."

"I'm interested in a cabin by the lake, probably the same as everyone else. I hear they don't come up for sale very often." I replied.

"You're right there," she said. "There are only two that I know of and, oddly enough, they are next door to each other."

"Really. That is odd. What do you think is the reason? Is there a feud or something? Don't want to get involved in anything like that."

"Oh, no," she replied. "In one case, the owner passed away and the children are fighting over the property. Probably not really for sale until that is cleared up anyway. The other, the owner, well the owner, had an unfortunate accident. His wife has put the property up for sale."

She looked as if she had revealed enough information and backed away, looking for something to do. I lingered over my coffee and bagel and tuned up my ears. Being old folks, the other customers' hearing wasn't as good as mine, and their whispering was loud.

"Suppose he doesn't know about Steve's death, accident, suicide, whatever it was."

"Too bad about that," one remarked. "Shame Nora wants to sell. Thinks she is too good for this town now. Heard she never looks anyone up or comes into town unless she can't help it."

"Talks to nobody in town now except the sheriff. Her father died a couple of years ago. Folks say she didn't visit him much before he died anyway," said another."

"Sure seems funny, Steve drowning. Never hear much about anyone drowning in that small lake. Sure seems peculiar. Do you think it was an accident? Suicide? Do you think...?" And they continued their debate.

"Oh, did she?" asked one old-timer."

"No way," said another."

"I heard him say that," someone else commented.

"Oh, don't listen to them," the waitress commented. "My name is Lisa, and these oldsters regurgitate the local news every day in here, and this drowning accident gives them a lot to chew on," she offered. "Where are you from?"

"San Francisco, and yes, I knew Steve. What do you think? About the accident, I mean." I asked, looking up at her from the counter. She was a woman in her fifties, I supposed, with dark brown hair that was obviously dyed, judging by the lock of gray hair emerging at the base of her short hairdo. I wondered if she had always lived here. Probably was the answer I gave to myself.

After Lisa placed the old-fashioned glass coffee pot back on the burner, she turned back to me and answered me directly.

"I think a lot of shenanigans went on with that snooty San Francisco group that descended upon the town whenever they wanted. The sheriff catered to them and they ignored us as if we weren't here until they needed something. Nora, the drowning victim's wife who used to be a local, included herself in that snobby group since her marriage to Steve. Steve himself was a nice guy who sometimes even came in here and had a cup of coffee and chatted with whoever was here. Shame about him dying. But an accident is just that, an accident." Lisa continued. "I don't give it much thought or make anything more out of it. That's just my opinion. But I do think it was very odd."

After concluding such a lengthy dissertation, she went back to looking busy, checking a small amount of receipts. I didn't suppose she wanted any further conversation, or my opinion on the matter, so

I finished my cup of coffee, left a five-dollar bill on the counter, and moved toward the door saying goodbye to the old fellows and their one female counterpart on my way out. The elderly woman tugged at my jacket as I passed her on the way to the door, obviously wanting to ask me something. So I stopped.

"Say fella, are you thinking of making an offer on that cabin?"

"Don't know yet," I replied when I turned around to face her.

"Well, my name is Mrs. McGuire, Mary to my friends, and if you decide to buy, I would surely be interested in the antiques in that old place," she proposed, and stood up and thrust out her business card from deep inside her coat. "I own the only antiques and collectibles store here in town."

The guys laughed, and one said, "Junk is what I call the stuff, but city people sometimes buy anything old."

Mrs. McGuire just ignored the comment and continued chatting. "I think that old cabin probably has a lot of stuff inside that I am certain Nora would just throw away. I would really like the first chance at bidding on it."

"Sure, I will keep that in mind," I replied, putting her card in a pocket I never used.

"My name is Charlie," said one of the old men at the wooden table, "and I own the only auto shop in town, but I don't have a card. This old fellow sitting next to me is Phil, who used to own the only gas station in town. Gas prices are high here, and you don't get many customers. Nora's father used to work for Phil in the old days. Phil was just telling the guys here, including Mary, that he recalled a conversation he accidentally overheard between Frank and Steve. They didn't see him in the next room and were standing in front of the counter...talking really loudly."

"Tell him what Frank said," Charlie interrupted.

"I am. I am. I take my time," Phil said in an angry tone. "Give me time."

"Well," Phil began again after a sip of his coffee, Frank had the louder voice. He said, "I've given you a lot of leeway over the years, Steve, because of our friendship. But this is too much."

"Did you find out what 'too much' was?" I asked credulously, realizing I also had interrupted Phil.

"Nope," he answered dejectedly, putting his coffee cup down. "But I have to tell you, I never went along with the village feeling that Steve was such a nice guy. I think he was a fake."

"Why do you say that?" I asked.

"Just think so…always have," Phil said.

"The others looked at each other as in a conspiracy, and Charlie said, "Phil has always professed that, but he has no proof at all."

Phil continued his pronouncement. "Steve was always on stage, if you know what I mean. He always said what was expected of him, just the right thing like a politician. Always flattering the ladies, complimenting the men, and chatting with the locals. Don't think he was sincere."

"Gordon came into my store once," piped in the elderly gentleman sitting next to Charlie. "Bart's the name," he said and shook my hand across the table.

"A real dandy Gordon was," he said. "I own…owned the only drugstore in this town. Gordon came into my store one day. Forgot his toiletry bag, he said, and looked around for at least fifteen minutes huffing and puffing and muttering to himself the whole time. He was mostly complaining about the lack of selection. He was apparently oblivious of the fact I could hear every word since he was the only customer in the store. Finally, Gordon came up to me at the pharmacy counter and inquired about our very best body lotion for men.

"Body lotion for a man! Imagine! I told him that we didn't have too many requests for that product in this town, so I didn't carry much of a selection. Gordon huffed again and bought a little sample and a few other items. Not much. Then he left my store without as much as a goodbye or thank you for the help. He just paid and left. Quite an irritable chap.

"How did I know who he was, you might ask? Charlie had described him and his attitude many times at coffee." Then Bart laughed a big resounding laugh and signaled to Lisa for a refill. She came over to the table and added her comments since she had been listening from her place behind the counter.

"Gordon wouldn't stop in here—no way—no lattes. But I have seen him in the street. Dressed like he was walking about in San Francisco. Not like Steve," she said while pouring a refill for Bart and others. "Steve could be seen in his red plaid shirt when he was in town. Everyone knew when he walked down the street. It was his signature look. I guess that is what San Franciscans imagine men wear here all the time in the Sierras. He wore it like a uniform."

That damn red flannel shirt. It has popped up again. Phil continued chattering on, ignoring the bored stares of his companions. I stopped listening and remembered my impression of Steve in college, and even the impression Steve made on me when I saw him again in San Francisco.

Steve would have made a good politician.

I caught the end of Phil's diatribe. "Always made himself known," growled Phil. "Driving through town in his big fancy truck. Could be he was running away from financial troubles."

"I'm sure Nora costs a lot to maintain," chimed in Mrs. McGuire laughing. "She loves spending money. To think her dad was a simple auto mechanic in this town."

In my thoughts, I remembered one of my favorite sayings, "Don't be fooled by people who look like they are rich; they may just have a lot of debt."

"I'm sure the cabin is paid for, at least," I offered weakly.

"Don't be foolish," warned Phil. "I'm talking about their business and home in San Francisco."

I thought of Steve, Gordon, and our meeting at the cabin, and why I thought I was called to visit as a financial counselor. It did seem they were having money difficulties, according to their argument. I thought it best to keep this knowledge to myself.

"I had better get going. I'm off to the realty office."

"Don't be too upset by Phil's comments. As a retired guy, he has a lot of time to wonder about such things. Come again for a chat. Lisa lets us sit here every day and visit," commented Charlie.

As I jingled through the door, I decided that as an outsider I would probably be the next topic of conversation. Lisa would surely love telling them I was from San Francisco, and they would savor the tidbit about my being there the night of Steve's death. But I learned something from them, too. It wasn't just me questioning the way in which Steve died.

# Twenty-two

At the realty office, I told the salesperson I was a friend of Nora's, which I was, and that I wasn't sure about buying the cabin and didn't want any pressure from Nora. I asked for her silence, even keeping my being in town from the sheriff who, after all, was a friend of Nora's. I told the realtor I wanted to make a decision on my own. She agreed to keeping my appearance in town a secret, hopeful for a future sale.

When I arrived at the cabin, it looked the same as it had before I knocked at the door that first day. I did not intend to stay there overnight but had gotten the keys. I told the realtor I would be staying the weekend at the inn instead.

I headed first for the shed. I don't know why, but I thought some clue might still be there. Call it intuition, but I was convinced there were still clues that could resolve the indecision behind Steve's death being an accident or a suicide.

I opened the door to the shed and entered to scrounge through its contents, hopeful for no further intrusion from the neighbor. I figured he knew my car by now and, after all, I had permission to be there. I took my time. The contents were the same: boat, motor, life jackets, fishing equipment, cans for gas, etc. But this time, I was not in haste and took my time. I didn't know what I was looking for, but I figured I would know when I found it.

And I found it.

Under the stuff piled in the boat was the red flannel shirt, the very same shirt Steve wore that night when I saw him walking out to the lake in the moonlight. It was clean with no dirt or torn spots.

How could that be? If I saw Steve walking out to the lake at midnight wearing that red plaid shirt, and he drowned in the lake, how could that same shirt be in the shed not soiled or torn?

My questions racing around my head like crazy, I decided to walk again to the spillway. I walked a short way down the path when I suddenly decided to stray off it. I scrambled up the boulders in a small glacial area until I came to a vantage point overlooking the lake. I came upon a side path which I had not seen before. It was a trail, probably made by locals over some time. It led to another dirt road wide enough for four-wheel vehicles or motorcycles. This trail also led to the spillway.

Perhaps Steve could have walked to the spillway, met someone with a car or motorcycle and driven away. If Steve had developed such a plan, then who was his accomplice? What went wrong? Was his death an accident?

I heard a motorcycle driving to the spillway. A young man with his girlfriend riding behind him stopped near me and looked somewhat surprised at my being there.

"A great spot," I said, as if I had known about it for years."

"Usually private," he replied. "Outsiders rarely discover it. Everyone in town knows about it, however. You were smart to find it."

He walked away with his girlfriend, and after a few minutes they left, probably in search of a different private spot.

I peered over the spillway, thinking back to when I first saw it from the trail walkway. Then, I'd seen it from the official access road with the searchers and the sheriff. I was puzzled by Steve accidentally falling into the spillway or the lake. What was it? He had some marijuana in his blood. Did he fall? Lots of questions took my attention away. Most pressing question of all, how did he die?

# Twenty-three

I turned to walk away and saw a man about ten yards from me just staring. My pulse quickened, and my fight or flight reflex kicked in. He didn't move, and I wasn't sure what move I should make next, when he spoke.

"What are you doing here?" he asked.

"What are YOU doing here?" I replied.

"I have a reason to be here. My name is Paul Smith and I am an insurance investigator looking into a recent claim of an accident," he said.

"I have been trying to talk with you, but your office said you were unavailable and couldn't talk with me unless I was related to Steve," I said.

"How did you know I am investigating that accident?" Paul asked.

"Why, are there others that occurred here? I was here when they found Steve," I said.

Paul stood for a few moments, and then loosened up and walked toward me in a friendlier manner.

"I'm sorry, but I am not really supposed to be talking with just anyone about the investigation," Paul said. "But off the record, since I heard from the sheriff you have been doing some questioning on your own, perhaps we can share information. Strictly off the record."

"Sure," I said, eager for any information I could get. "If I were Steve, I would have taken my money from the bank, met someone here at the access road, and disappeared into a new life."

"Not that easy an answer," Paul said. "Too many loose ends."

"Like what?" I asked.

"Like, there wasn't that much money in his bank account, not enough for him and especially not enough for his wife," Paul offered.

I smiled at that remark.

"Steve did die from drowning because at the autopsy the local coroner discovered his lungs were filled with water. But the coroner didn't uncover any obvious marks of an accident that would cause him to become unconscious, fall into the lake and drown," Paul remarked.

"What are you implying?" I asked.

"I am investigating the possibility someone killed him intentionally," Paul said without emotion.

Stunned, I couldn't say anything for a few moments. So far, that possibility had only occurred in my imagination.

"For what reason?" I persisted.

"The insurance money being the obvious one, of course. There could be others we don't know about."

"Who besides Steve's wife and Gordon could be involved? Perhaps Gordon and Nora were having an affair?" I suggested.

"Gordon certainly is very protective of Nora. I learned that, and that he has quite a temper," Paul commanded.

Yes, he does have quite a temper.

"You are aware the sheriff and Nora go way back," he added.

"Yes," I replied.

"Well, did you know they still see each other when Nora comes to town?"

"I heard she doesn't come often," I said in her defense.

"But when she does," said Paul, "Nora has been spotted at Frank's house. The neighbors told me. They have seen her also with her brother Bobby, and Frank has not been active in pursuing convictions involving her brother's drug dealings either."

"And getting back to Gordon, what about him? What else have you discovered besides his bad temper," I asked.

"His history with Nora is not as long as her relationship with Frank, but intense. Did you know it was Nora who convinced Steve to have Gordon become his partner?"

I nodded yes, as I didn't want him to think this information exchange was one-sided.

"Maybe you don't know the full extent of their history. At first, Gordon was a more exciting prospect than Steve, but Nora didn't count on Steve's spending. Steve was as extravagant as Nora when it came to money," Paul shared.

The investigator stepped back on the rocky ledge and continued his dialogue. "The mortgage on the house in Marin is in the thousands monthly, and Steve owed everyone. Gordon, on the other hand, is conservative when it comes to money. Gordon's import/export business seems to be thriving. Some wonder why."

"Does he import or export drugs?" I wondered aloud.

Paul paused for a moment and then answered, "We haven't found that out...but perhaps.

"Gordon has always wanted to be close to Nora. He has become something of a protector to her, and Steve either seemed oblivious of this or just didn't care. Gordon was included in their circle of intimate friends as well as Beth and her husband. They were seen together, all of them, on multiple occasions. From what I could gather, Nora seemed to be having an affair with someone, but I haven't figured out who it was yet," mused the investigator, more or less to himself.

"I shouldn't have said that. It is confidential. Hell, everything is confidential. You won't say anything, will you?" he asked. "I want to keep my job, but you could be helpful. I am having trouble with this investigation. On that night, did you really identify Steve who left the cabin, or could it have been someone else such as Gordon wearing Steve's shirt?"

I was surprised by his question. Surely, it was Steve. He had on the same red flannel shirt he had worn at dinner, but I did only see the back of his shirt and Steve and Gordon were about the same height.

"I guess it could have been Gordon," I said, remembering the clean shirt in the shed.

"Then you didn't hear him get up or a door close or any other noise except the garbage cans?" Paul asked.

"No."

"You don't even know if Gordon was asleep in the cabin then?"

"No," I said again, thinking back to the episode "Gordon had said earlier he would take a sleeping pill or listen to music with earplugs because he had difficulty falling asleep. I assumed he was sleeping when I heard the garbage cans."

"Now tell me, what do you know?" Paul asked.

"I just found the red flannel shirt I saw Steve wearing the night he left the cabin. I found it in the storage shed. But that can't be the same shirt he was wearing when they found his body at the dam. That one would be soiled and torn. Also, the cranky old man who lives next door to Steve's cabin told me he witnessed Steve returning from the dock about midnight. That can't be right. I heard the garbage cans rattle at midnight because I looked at my bedside clock and saw Steve walking outside."

"That old man didn't tell me all that. He could have been wrong about the time, but that doesn't explain the shirt, or the direction Steve was headed," Smith said. "By the way, are you staying here long?"

"Just a couple of days or less. Can't get this episode out of my life yet. Just want it resolved. Shouldn't be meddling, I guess," I whimpered.

"Well, I think you have a good eye for detail...I like that. Take my card. Call me if you learn anything new. I'll call you at the inn if I discover anything. If you want, give me your cell phone as well," Paul urged, handing me his business card.

"That's an excellent thought," I said, scribbling my cellphone number on a scrap of paper. After I gave it to him, we both left the scene, and I headed back to the inn to a ringing land phone in my room. It was Frank, and this time he wasn't so friendly.

"I thought you would stop by my office if you came to town," Frank said sharply.

"Hello yourself, sir."

"I'm taking a ride up to Kennedy Meadows late this afternoon to check on something. Why don't you ride along with me and we can talk. At least I'll know where you are," Frank offered. "I'll pick you up in a few minutes in the parking lot outside the inn."

I agreed, reluctantly. I wanted to talk with him, too, but I didn't relish a confrontation.

I lay on the bed, thinking. I couldn't seem to put all the pieces together, and I knew I didn't have all of them. It was becoming evident there was a lot about this intimate group I didn't understand.

I began to wonder if I'd been dealt certain cards to play, and this intimate group of friends wasn't too happy with the way I was playing. I wasn't following their script. Maybe I was supposed to play the expendable witness. The hair stood up on the back of my neck.

If there were two shirts, my report was critical. I was going to give Frank my information and then go home. But could Frank be involved too? If I go to Kennedy Meadows with him, I might wind up just as dead as poor Steve. But I don't like being treated as a fool, I told myself, my eyes hardening into a squint.

I heard the honking of Frank's jeep in the parking lot. Too late for a convenient escape. I gathered my courage and went out to face him. As I got into his jeep, feeling like a lamb being led to the slaughter, my decision wavered, but I had already decided on this approach. As I fastened my seat belt, I inwardly prayed that I had made the right decision.

### *Twenty-four*

Frank started the journey by continuing on Highway 108 as it left Sugar Pine and climbed upward on its path to the mountains, but the highway narrowed considerably as it rose. The curves in the road were accentuated, and we gained altitude quickly. The Sierras are beautiful but deadly. Many climbers, skiers, as well as drivers have found this to be true. The vistas are incredible, but the road hugs the side of the mountain as you drive, and the edge of the road descends quickly. I was the passenger, and although I knew the sheriff was well aware of its dangers, he was angry and driving a bit too fast.

"What did you hope to gain from coming here without even telling me?" Frank asked, his eyes going squinty. "I really don't know why you are so involved. I'm beginning to wonder about your motives!"

"I don't know why I can't just forget the incident. Being here when Steve died makes it personal for me," I replied. "I just want some answers. No...I really need some answers."

"It's very personal for me, too," Frank said, "Steve was my friend as well, and it's my job to find out what happened to him."

We continued a few more breathtaking miles before Frank spoke again.

"I told you that Nora, Steve, and I all knew each other from when we were younger. I told you Nora lived with her father and brother, and that her father died years ago. Her brother stayed here in Sugar Pine. Bobby chose to live a rather unconventional life and make money in unconventional ways. Do I make myself clear? I have ignored him, for Nora's sake, and besides, he is not in my jurisdiction anymore. He lives further up in another county. I do hear about Bobby from time to time. That's where we're headed right now, to his cabin," Frank told me.

"What do you hope to learn?"

"I don't know, but I thought I would check on him and keeping you near me would be better than having you meddle all over town. The ride will do you good, anyway."

Surprisingly, around one particular curve lay a lovely meadow, green and flat, with tourist cabins situated across the highway. "Does he live here?" I asked.

"No, not permanently, but from time to time he lives behind the cabins. Too many people for Bobby to stay here long. Bobby likes more solitude."

We continued driving on the highway for a few more miles until a side road appeared and Frank veered off, following the road for a while. It was a dirt road, not maintained, and very bumpy. Steve steered around the bumps as if he did this often, and we passed a few cabins as we inched along. They were small and slapped together with odd remnants of wood decorating the front yard alongside piles of rubbish, old car parts, and, in some cases, even old cars.

"Don't usually show this place to tourists, I bet," I remarked sarcastically.

"There are many kinds of people who live in the mountains," Frank commented. "Some live here full time because they like its peacefulness, then there are tourists who come here annually because of its natural beauty, and then there are those who are hiding away. Bobby is one of the latter."

Just then we came to nearly the end of the road, and Frank stopped in front of yet another scruffy cabin. "Stay in the jeep," he ordered, and I decided this time I'd best follow his commands without questioning.

I watched as Frank skillfully maneuvered around the loose junk outside the cabin and knocked loudly at the front door. When no one answered, Frank went around to the back of the cabin while I locked the doors of the jeep to ensure my security.

After what seemed like an eternity, Frank appeared inside the cabin at the door with a rather short, gaunt man with a beard. The young man was wearing a flannel shirt like Steve's, but this one was old and worn and a different color. I could hear the two of them shouting at each other.

"None of your business," the young man who appeared to be Bobby shouted. "You can't do anything about me up here."

"I can tell my suspicions to the local authorities who can do something about it," Frank replied loudly.

I was fearful there might be a physical confrontation, but Bobby only shoved Frank once, and Frank restrained himself from responding in a like manner. Maybe that's why Frank had me come along, as a witness.

As Frank retreated, Bobby slammed his front door; and Frank walked back to the jeep and gave me a funny look as I fumbled to unlock the driver side. He drove back to the main highway without saying anything. When we started driving back toward Sugar Pine, I thought it was time to start asking some questions, but he spoke first.

"Bobby claims he only knew of Steve's death when he got a newspaper one day down at the grocery store. He claims Nora never even called him or tried to contact him, even though he does have a land phone up here. That explanation doesn't ring true." Frank concentrated on driving.

Going downhill on the highway was even more frightening than uphill. Now the passenger side hugged the cliffs, and I tried to focus on the road just in front of us. I decided not to carry on much of a conversation until we got back to his office. But once again, it was the sheriff who began to chat.

"I hate it when there is someone right behind me," he said, looking into his rear-view mirror.

I looked back to see a large, red truck closing down on us from behind. My heart leaped at the sight. I really hate it when someone is tailgating-me on a windy road, and I sympathized with Frank. Hopefully, it was not a fast driver who thought himself invincible.

"It is coming awfully fast," remarked Frank calmly.

I thought quite possibly the driver was stupid and didn't know he was tailgating an officer of the law. The driver would certainly feel foolish as he got closer. But instead of backing off the accelerator, the driver increased his speed as he got closer.

"Get the license plate," Frank yelled at me.

I scrambled around looking for something to write with and found scraps of paper and a pen in the cup holder. When I looked back, the truck started to race past us, and I was able to see the number and view its driver clearly. The man was wearing a cowboy hat sloped over his head, a heavy jacket, and dark glasses. I was too scared to notice anything else. I was more fearful for my life.

Frank's grip on the steering wheel was tight. He stared out the rearview mirror for a few seconds, and then fought to keep his jeep on the road. It wasn't easy. At every turn, the other driver swerved next to us, trying to drive us over the cliff. The driver missed a few times, and then, thankfully, another car suddenly approached from the oncoming direction. Our pursuer slid back behind us and when the oncoming car went by, gave up and passed us, continuing ahead. Frank pulled over on a scenic overpass, killing the engine. We sat there in a cloud of dust, as the red truck sped out of view.

"Are you all right?" Frank asked.

Shaking with fear, I said, "I think so. But I may never want to drive this road again."

"Don't blame you; that was frightening even for me."

"Was that Bobby?" I asked.

"No. It didn't look like him. Probably one of his pothead friends trying to warn me not to interfere with their activities. Hope you got the license plate so we can find out," Frank said.

"I got it," I said, catching my breath and sighing in relief.

We didn't talk anymore on the way back to town. Finally, we reached Sugar Pine, and Frank took me to his office to do the paperwork on the incident. I handed over the slip of paper, and he sat at his desk-to check the license plate number.

Julie was visibly upset by our story and kept mothering me with coffee and water and whatever else she could think of in an attempt to be helpful. With Julie knowing about the incident, I knew the whole town would learn of it by evening.

"Well, damn!" Frank muttered, sitting at his computer. "That license plate is a dead end. It probably replaced the original one and the fake license plate probably has been used many times over. I'm pretty sure it couldn't have been Bobby."

# Twenty-five

After apologizing for involving me in such an incident, Frank dropped me off at the inn. He said we could talk later, and I agreed. I went straight to my room and laid down on the bed for a while, but it was claustrophobic to be in that small room after what had just happened, and my mind was reeling with the latest event. I decided to go to the bar and found it almost empty except for the waiter, who was also the barkeeper, Kit.

"What will you have?" Kit asked. "Hey! You're the guy I talked with earlier, and the one who the sheriff was with this afternoon! You two nearly had an accident on the highway. Is that right?"

"Well, I wouldn't exactly call it an accident. Wow, news really travels fast in this town!"

"Lisa told me after Julie called her," Kit said, summoning a woman who had been sitting at a table in the restaurant away from my view. I recognized her as the waitress from the coffee shop. "Come on over, Lisa."

After exchanging pleasantries, we got right down to the gossip while I drank my beer.

"Bobby always was a bad seed. The older folks here said he was headed the wrong way even as a child. They said he would come to no good. His sister Nora, on the other hand, apparently made it in the big city, but she didn't come too often to visit here except when she brought her rich friends from Marin. She stopped mixing with the locals, except for the sheriff. The old guys down at the coffee shop said they had spotted Bobby in town lately and were worried why he was here. They also spotted Nora a couple of times, which as I said, is unusual, but after Steve's death, she probably had to come to sell the cabin."

She is telling me a lot more than she had revealed in front of the elderly locals who met daily at the coffee shop.

I took out my wallet to indicate I needed to pay my bill and leave and the two photos I had found at the cabin earlier fell out on to the counter. Lisa picked them up for me and looked at them closely.

"That's Steve and Nora, and their friends Beth and her husband, Jim," I said.

"I recognize Steve and Nora, of course, but I don't recognize the other man and woman. But this second man was spotted in town a couple of times with Nora."

She was pointing to Jim, Beth's husband. I was surprised. It did seem unusual, but in the event of Steve's death and perhaps, if Gordon was busy, Jim might have helped her with the details here in Sugar Pine. Then again, the photo was old.

"What can you tell me about Bobby?" I asked. "What kind of problems does he have?"

"The usual sort of problems nobody talks about...minor drug offenses, drunken driving, that kind of thing. He keeps to himself mostly and does odd jobs if the person doesn't know his history. Some people that do know him feel sorry for him and give him jobs, like the manager of the tourist cabins up the road from here. That way the manager thinks he can keep an eye on him and be safe as well. From the description of the truck, I don't think Bobby was the one who tried to run you both off the road," Lisa said.

"Are Bobby and his sister on good terms?" I asked.

"Not really. Nora was only spotted with him recently. Maybe she was helping him with groceries and such. Maybe Bobby was doing odd jobs at the cabin. Don't really know. When Nora came to town she was always dressed up and looking like she was doing us a favor by being here."

"Thanks," I said and paid for the beer.

As usual, my conversations in this town always seemed to have the effect of producing more questions than answers. I went back to my room with all kinds of thoughts rolling around in my brain.

Why was Jim with Nora? What involvement did Bobby have in this business? For that matter, what involvement did the sheriff have with Steve's death? Were drugs a part of the whole mess?

I didn't think I would sleep well that night.

# Twenty-six

That same evening, the sheriff called to ask if we could put off having dinner together until the next night, as he had a lot of "investigating" to do. He told me not to do any of my own without him. That was his job, Frank said. I could play with my laptop instead. "And, stay out of trouble!"

The internet is filled with endless sources of information, some helpful, some useless, and some downright silly. But having little else to do, I entered cyberspace on my laptop which I had brought with me to fill my time. I had brought some sandwiches to my room.

I looked up Sugar Pine and the dam, but only learned that the annual "Founder's Day" would be held on this weekend starting Friday with a large, outdoor barbecue featuring a spicy chili contest. The list of events included an antique fair, arts and crafts displays, and a carnival event for the children. The local Chamber of Commerce, it seemed, hoped to bring more tourists to town early before the usual season began.

The small lake created by the dam had its own website featuring the rental cabins, the campground, and the lake's activities, which included boat rentals. The website included a map showing the trailhead around the lake. The map did not show the unofficial access road where I had talked with the investigator.

Then I looked up Stanislaus National Forest where Sugar Pine, the lake, and Kennedy Meadows were located and studied the road off Highway 108 where Bobby lived. Then I tried to research Bobby, but without police records available to me, I couldn't find anything.

Because I ran out of ideas for research, I googled both Steve and Gordon. Steve was listed for some buildings his company had constructed in Marin and some charity events in which he had been involved. Gordon was listed for the same charity events, but also for being a prominent importer and exporter in San Francisco. He also was listed as a benefactor for local artists.

Having worked on Nora's personal assets and knowing of some of Steve's business affairs, I knew they weren't rolling in money, but Gordon seemed to be doing very well. What was Gordon exporting and importing besides antiques? Could Gordon be involved in drugs?

My imagination is getting the best of me.

As a healthier diversion, I looked up more about Sugar Pine. Seems as if it was called Strawberry Lake in the past, so named for the wild strawberries that grew there in the time of the Mi-Wuk Indians. Actually a small dam, sitting just above the Sierra foothills off highway 108, it was originally built for mining and hydroelectric power, but now was used primarily for recreational purposes. It was located on the south fork of the Stanislaus River in the huge Stanislaus National Forest which was created in 1891.

Strawberry Lake, as I would call it now, seemed diminutive in this huge forest. Its location was special because of its accessibility off Highway 108. Most other small bodies of water were hidden in the forest and not seen by most tourists. Apparently further north, Highway 108 crossed between two distinct wildernesses and reached the peak at Sonora Pass at an elevation over 9,000 feet. The information about the pass included a warning not to attempt driving it on a snowy day as parts of the highway would be closed.

By then I was very tired. I looked at the bedside clock and realized it was too late for a real meal and, besides, I had eaten lots of stale peanuts with a beer. I was more tired than hungry, and decided I needed rest. Still wearing my clothes, I fell into a tired sleep, but at least I didn't have nightmares, as I thought I might.

## *Twenty-seven*

The next morning, I woke up groggy to a knock at my door which startled me. I bolted up to answer it. It was Frank, anxious to see if I was staying put and not stirring up trouble. Maybe he also wants to know if I am safe, I hoped.

"Yes, Frank" I said dryly, "I overslept this morning, but now I need to get out of this room, have some breakfast, and breathe some the fresh air.

"Well, you've slept past breakfast time here at the inn," Frank said.

"Guess I have to exchange gossip at the coffee shop instead.

"And I thought you might get bored in this small berg, you being from the big city and all. Go see your friends at the coffee shop, but no investigating. Just listen," Frank commanded.

"Or I thought I might drive to Sonora Pass," I said half kiddingly.

There were a few moments of hesitation on the part of the sheriff. His face was sterner and as he turned away to walk to his jeep, he suddenly stopped and turned back to address me.

"Well," said Frank slowly. "I do have to visit the ranger at the station about a mile from here and may have to drive beyond that. I guess having you with me is better than having you wander off alone. I will pick you up at two o'clock. Be ready."

"Or perhaps I'll just take my car. I really would like to see the mountain pass while I'm here," I said.

"All right. I can go further. Just be ready," said the sheriff impatiently, as if addressing a cranky child. "I promise it won't be as exciting this time."

After he left, the phone rang. It was Paul, the insurance investigator. He had more questions.

"How did Steve seem when you ran into him that day in the restaurant in San Francisco?" Paul asked.

"Steve seemed happy, friendly, and just the same as he was in college."

"Did he talk about any problems at all?"

"No, as a matter of fact, he said his business was doing quite well. When he took me to lunch after that first time we bumped into each other, he spent money as liberally as he had in college. I would have to say Steve appeared not to have any financial problems. I only found out later that he did."

"You said Nora has hired you to help with her finances. I know you probably can't divulge much, but just answer yes or no if you want. Does she appear to have any problems?" Paul asked.

"I can answer that question easily," I replied. "We haven't quite signed any agreement yet, but I have been looking into her personal finances, not the business. Although it is a lesser amount, it all looks fine. I'm sure you already know she returned the money Steve withdrew from the bank before he died."

"Yes, that whole business was odd, though."

"In what way?" I asked.

"Well," he paused, probably trying to determine whether he should tell me. "If it was a suicide, why would he take out money? Also, I have witnesses saying Bobby and Steve had been seen together earlier the week Steve died. Bobby, as I am sure you know from your experience yesterday, was on the other side of the law.

"I'm inclined to think that somehow Bobby is involved in all of this. Nora says she knows nothing of her brother and Steve being together. But I don't believe her," Paul said.

There was a pause on his end of the line. I didn't want to press him. I thought he might stop giving me information if I asked too many questions, so I just stayed quiet. I wanted him to continue, and he did.

"Frank and I have decided to question him further. I understand you have met Bobby. Quite a character. He is not like Nora at all. Not as attractive, not as bright, and keeps to himself mostly," Paul said.

"I never met Bobby. I just might have seen him from the window of the sheriff's jeep," I confessed.

"It doesn't matter. We'll keep the same deal. You tell me what you learn, and I will do likewise," Paul continued. "Keep in touch. If you find out anything, call me. Normally I don't involve outsiders in my investigations, but you might hear something from that little group of friends that could help me."

The more I learned about this intimate group, the more surprised I had become. Back in San Francisco, the old college friend I ran into had remembered parties with Steve at the cabin to which I had never been invited. I guessed I was too straight. They recalled not only Nora hanging on the outskirts of these parties at first, but also her brother, Bobby. It was her brother who supplied them with weed, and the sheriff, although he didn't smoke, had a drinking problem and was often passed out. Apparently, after Steve's wife died, Steve came to the cabin sometimes to rest and relax by himself. According to them, Nora stepped up her attention to Steve and I knew the rest of the story. I found this occurred at about the time Frank was elected sheriff. Was that a coincidence?

The investigator commented, "Are you still there?"

I was off in my own thoughts. "Yeah, yeah." I was surprised when he continued asking for my help.

"I do need more information right now. I'm stuck. Nora's lawyer is pressing for a conclusion to this case and so is my boss. I'll talk to you later."

After he hung up and I thought about what he had said, I came up with yet another question, but decided not to call him back just then. Was Steve meeting someone when he went out that night? If so and his death was an accident, who was it, and why were there no bruises on his body? How did the boat get back to the shed?

# Twenty-eight

I had decided, before my drive with the sheriff, I would sneak off to the bait shop. I walked over to the lodge and when I got there, I noticed the shops were mostly void of tourists. I stopped at the small grocery store and picked up a sweet roll, sandwich, a drink, and some snack bars for later. Outside the store, I managed to eat all but the snack bars because I was hungry. I entered the bait shop and found there was only a young man behind the counter reading a fishing magazine. He looked up as I entered and asked me what I needed.

"Is there good fishing at this lake?" I asked, "What is being caught here?"

"The lake is planted with rainbow and brown trout, catfish, and even sometimes Kohanee salmon. Trout is always planted weekly during the summer months when kids are here and want to catch something."

Planted fish was a term I found amusing. I always thought people fished for wild ones in the streams and lakes. The idea of stocking a lake with fish only for recreational purposes was a weird concept for me.

I was looking around the small store when the clerk cleared his throat as if to signal it was time to buy, if I wanted to buy something. So I questioned more about the lake instead without looking too much like a novice fisherman.

"Where is the best place to fish?"

"Well," he said without hesitation, anxious to show his knowledge, "There are many good places to fish depending on what kind of fisherman you are." He waited for my reply.

I thought about Steve and what Gordon said about his fishing.

"I can fish anywhere," I responded. What am I saying? I don't know the first thing about fishing. "Just happen to be here today and find myself with time on my hands."

"Here's a printout of the lake and the fishing areas," the young man said, as he reached below the counter and pulled out a black and white Xerox. "As you can see, if you have a boat, the trolling is best in the deeper part of the lake shown here." He pointed to the middle of the lake indicated in a dark blue. "But the best possible fishing without anyone around is on the east side. You have to walk the loop trail to get there, but it's worth it for the solitude.

"Most tourists never go there. You can also fish from shore, of course, anywhere on the lake except in the swimming area at the beach. Near the big boulders at the north end of the lake off the same marked trail, and the rocky area near the cabins southwest of the dam are good places to fish."

"Does anyone fish near the dam?" I asked.

"Sure, but not on the dam. Some fish near the shore on both ends before the walkway across it," he replied.

"Is it dangerous?" I asked.

"No," he chuckled, 'not unless you throw yourself off the bridge and onto the spillway!"

Obviously, the police weren't passing along details of Steve's death. Bad for tourism. I thought of Steve and his so-called accident. He seemed to prefer fishing from a boat even though he couldn't swim, so he obviously trolled in the middle of the lake that, according to the map, narrowed and whose water was drawn into the dam. But the boat was in the shed with his life jacket and even his red flannel shirt.

"Are you going fishing today?" asked the clerk, startling me out of my thoughts.

"Not today, I guess. I just realized I really don't have the time, and I don't want to purchase new equipment and a license just for an hour or so," I said, "Maybe tomorrow."

The clerk was relieved, went back to reading his fishing magazine, and I wandered back to my motel room to wait for the sheriff. Sitting in a motel room is not my favorite activity, especially since it was so beautiful outside. But now the sheriff was only minutes away from coming. I wanted to look as if I had followed his orders and stayed at the inn since he'd left earlier.

# *Twenty-nine*

When the sheriff arrived, I shoved what food I had left into my pocket and walked with him to his jeep. Feeling very cooped up and needing some fresh air, I was anxious to get out on the road and away from my motel room.

The drive up 108 was spectacular and I was glad I had come along. According to the sheriff, most tourists that came to the lake never went beyond it as they were content with the beach, swimming, and boating. Also, many were put off by the narrow, winding road that gained altitude quickly and whose path looked straight down the mountain as a sheer drop. I was glad he was driving. I couldn't believe I was driving with Frank again on a treacherous road, but I was beginning to like the adrenalin it produced.

The sheriff chatted along the way like a tourist guide opening up about this beautiful area he obviously loved and probably the very reason that kept him here. We settled down to enjoy the scenery, while I enjoyed the fact he was driving and not me.

"Sorry about yesterday and even today," Frank remarked. "I have been a bit edgy since all of this happened, and I didn't mean to involve you in police matters. Hope today is better for both of us. Still looking for Bobby, and I am hoping our encounter will be friendlier if I do find him at home. Just want to check on a few details with him. Can't tell you about it, but just minor stuff about his whereabouts and his coming and goings to Sugar Pine. Just enjoy the ride.

"Strawberry Lake as the locals and I like to call it," Frank commented, "sits at about five thousand feet, but this narrow pass climbs up a five-mile gap between the glacial granite of the Carson-Iceberg Wilderness and the Emigrant Wilderness, and at its peak reaches over nine thousand feet. Quite an accomplishment," he said as he ended his tribute.

It really was an incredible view. Towering granite, multitudes of trees, and a brilliant blue sky that was unending. All of it produced a feeling of soaring in the clouds. At times, the windy road swerved and displayed a sheer drop down the canyon walls.

We stopped at the ranger station, but only briefly. Although the ranger was there, it was clear from their muted and short conversation, Frank hadn't gotten all the information he needed.

"We're going to drive to Kennedy Meadows further north just before the pass," he informed me. "Kennedy Meadows Pack Station is a major trailhead for hikes, both short and long ones, in the mountains. There is a rustic resort there with a small grocery store. Hikers can leave their stuff for a small fee before going out on the trails. They also have some cabins available from Memorial Day to early October before the snow falls and closes part of the highway. Some tourists even rent horses at the pack station.

"We have to take a spur road to the park there. Where we're going is across the highway to the trailhead. I need to talk with the manager, and you can walk around the store. Don't stray too far away, though. I don't want to have to go looking for you."

The sheriff addressed me like an errant youngster traveling with him. Again, I just ignored his remarks, but I felt like a child left alone for a few moments while Daddy took care of business. So after we got there, I wandered around the place. I felt as though I should be walking with my hands deep in my pockets.

The resort itself, as well as the grocery store, was indeed rustic. It looked like it belonged in the old West and was proud of it. Made from redwood, the primary building that housed the store was covered with posters, sayings, business cards, and lots of photos and notes left by hikers. I walked inside and immediately thought of a beer. There was an old-fashioned saloon next door and a cold beer sounded really good, even though it was early. They also had cold beer in the refrigerator, but I didn't think the sheriff would approve.

I settled on a candy bar, chips, and a small Coke. Great food choices lately, I thought. The sheriff had disappeared into a back room with the manager, and I could see them talking from the small crack in the door that had swung ajar. I couldn't hear what they said. However, when he returned, the sheriff looked disturbed. Frank offered some new information. "Bobby sometimes stays here in one of the cabins in the back, rent free as he repairs stuff for the manager and sometimes hauls supplies with his small truck. Bobby's truck is here, but he hasn't been seen for a day or so, best they can figure. Are you up for a short hike? I may know where he's camping, and I need to talk with him. We are still short of the pass itself, but after I talk with him, I promise I'll drive you there."

"Okay," I said, thinking this was a great opportunity to see the mountains, but as I looked down at my worn-out tennis shoes, and looked over at his sturdy hiking boots, I was somewhat worried.

Still talking, the sheriff strolled over to his jeep. "We'll take some water," Frank said as he lifted out a backpack from the back seat. "I know the trail well and I don't need a map."

I would love to have a map, I thought, but it's clear I am not going to have time to get one. Frank walked off quickly across the highway to a trailhead. I didn't want to complain, or he might just leave me at the pack station waiting for him.

I followed as Frank headed across the highway to a wooden marker that was the trailhead. I also noted one that pointed the way to Deadman Campground. That sign seemed a warning and gave me a chill.

We hiked on level ground for a while, for which I was grateful. Then we crossed a narrow footbridge over a river. So far, so good. When we reached a junction that seemed confusing, I was relieved when the sheriff, without any hesitation, headed left. He did seem to know the trail. Earlier, the sheriff had pointed out that the Mi-Wuk Indians marked their trails with dead skunks. I would have been happy with clearer directions on the wooden posts along the trail. They were small and some had been jostled so the arrows indicating direction were turned. The sheriff noted those that were wrong but didn't attempt to correct them.

We passed by a huge granite dome and suddenly the trail became steeper and rockier, but the sheriff never slowed his pace. His leadership skills were similar to a bad tourist guide marching ahead of his group without realizing the group behind wasn't keeping up, but I knew he wasn't going to slow his pace. I guessed this was a short walk in the mountains to him. Unlike him, I had no idea where we were going and really needed hiking boots.

I was tiring out and feeling the altitude. My breath was getting labored and my knees were failing me. I was definitely out of shape, and the sheriff seemed a good hiker. I was worried that for every step in this direction, we had to take one getting back out. But every time I was discouraged, something beautiful appeared on the trail, such as small cascading waterfalls. It was beautiful, but I was determined to find out just how far we were going. When we crossed yet another narrow footbridge, I finally asked, "Just how far are we hiking, Sheriff?"

He stopped abruptly as I undoubtedly had broken his concentration and reluctantly answered me. "Not too much further. We're coming to a small lake just ahead," Frank yelled back without slowing his fast pace.

I trudged along, aware I was only extra baggage, and we climbed a narrow, steep path that ended sharply on a small ridge overlooking an equally small lake.

"We're here," Frank announced.

It was like an unexpected jewel in a pile of stones. A small blue lake in a wide vista of green trees and blue sky.

"I have to go down there," said the sheriff pointing to the lake. "You can wait for me here." He stared at my shoes as if noticing them for the first time, which he probably was. "You're tired, anyway."

He set off at his usual fast pace down a narrow path whose rocks blew past him as he walked. I saw him disappear with some trepidation. After all, I had no idea where I was. I had left no information about my whereabouts with anyone, and the inn staff, and even Julie, didn't know where I had gone. The sheriff hadn't even introduced me to the ranger or the manager of the pack station at Kennedy Meadows. I decided to dismiss my paranoia concerning the sheriff and being left alone or worse in this vast wilderness and focus on something else.

I looked around at the forest. Frank told me earlier that trees grew here only at specific heights and certain conditions. This was an interesting fact of nature my business major college education somehow missed. He pointed out my favorite tree I had remarked upon at the dam, the Sugar Pine, and said it produced the longest pinecone of all the conifers in this area. It was a favorite of first-time visitors because it was so easy to identify. Kids especially liked discovering those big, oblong cones.

Plants too, had their preferences, Frank had informed me. Besides the wild strawberry, there was a plant that was the first that came up after the snow. In fact, it literally came out of the snow and was the first sign of spring. Frank had showed me a photo at his house. It was called a snowflower, for obvious reasons. Frank said that it has no leaves but pops up out of the snow with a bright red flower introducing spring to the mountains. This giant of a man had spoken almost poetically about the trees, the flowers, and the geologic formations. Frank seemed in love with the mountains, and although, admittedly, I wasn't entirely interested at first, he drew me into the subject with his enthusiasm.

# Thirty

Soon I grew tired of my diversion with nature and returned to my fear of having been left alone on this mountain. Just then, I heard the crackling of the small rocks on the trail disturbed by the sheriff's boots.

"I found something disturbing," Frank said grimly.

I immediately thought of bears, wild animals, etc., but what came next was even more unnerving.

"I found someone down at the lake."

"Who?" I asked.

"Nora's brother...but not alive," he said simply.

"Did he fall?" I asked. "Is that how he died?"

"Unlikely."

"Why is it unlikely," I asked.

"Because Bobby has a bullet hole in his chest," Frank replied.

I said nothing.

"We have to walk back and get help. I can't get reception on my cellphone this high in the mountains. The sooner we descend, the better," Frank said calmly. "Can you make it, or do you want to stay here and wait?"

I did not want to stay there by myself on this lonely ridge, waiting for what could be hours.

"I'm fine," I said trying to act calm. "Let's go."

As we headed back, Frank said nothing, and I was left with my suspicions and paranoid thoughts. When at times the trail looked different from before, I imagined the sheriff was luring me off into the woods someplace and my body would never be found.

When we got to the cascades at the first footbridge, Frank stopped abruptly.

"Why are we stopping?" I asked.

"I want to check on something," Frank said sharply. "Stay here."

"Why?"

"Just stay here!" the sheriff shouted, and he disappeared down a forgotten trail to the creek below.

I remained on the footbridge for a few moments, but my curiosity overcame me, and I slowly made my way down to where he stood. He was just staring at large granite boulders in the middle of the stream that blocked the oncoming water and created a large, deep pool. A rock betrayed me, and I slipped, ending up in a pile next to him. Frank grabbed me harshly and when I was on my feet again, he still had me in his grip. I thought he was pushing me into the river.

"Let go, let go!" I yelled at him.

The sheriff continued to hold me for a few seconds more and then, as if his concentration was broken, released me and walked back up to the footbridge.

I followed him after a moment, reluctantly, because I didn't know my way back and there was yet another footbridge ahead and the junction. But now I didn't trust him.

Frank didn't speak the rest of way down the trail, and when we finally made it back to the junction, he turned right, just as I thought he should, and I felt somewhat reassured.

"I can get reception now," Frank said and moved off from me for a private conversation that I hoped was to the authorities.

"I don't have jurisdiction here," Frank explained as we crossed the meadow to the pack station. To my relief, the ranger was waiting for us, and the two of them spoke briefly before we got back in the sheriff's jeep.

"We used to fish at that water hole as kids. It was a long time ago," were the only words he spoke to me on the way back. No mention was made of driving further on to the pass, but I did not want to go there now anyway. I was exhausted and confused and still apprehensive of the sheriff. I just wanted to get back to the inn and rest. When Frank left me at the parking lot of the inn, he called me back to the jeep and rolled down the window.

"You saw nothing and shouldn't be involved," said Frank. Then he sped off and I was left in the parking lot, alone, wondering if what I had seen was going to get me killed.

I headed straight for the bar, had a drink and a sandwich then stayed awhile to collect myself. Some of the locals started drifting in. Then a few musicians came in and set up their equipment. It seemed like everyone knew each other and there was a lot of hand shaking and back slapping as the crowd entered. One of the men slapped me on the back, almost causing me to bump my face onto the bar. I turned around to see a tall cowboy complete with a Stetson hat and a broad smile welcoming me to his hangout.

"Hear you're from San Francisco," the cowboy said, spewing out the name in a long phrase. "Hear you were a friend of Steve's? Any friend of Steve's is a friend of mine. Welcome! Steve used to buy the house a round of drinks when he came into town." He waited hopefully for me to offer.

"Just going back to my room. Sorry. Maybe another time," I said trying to get down off the bar stool but not having much luck as the cowboy was a big, broad man and he was blocking my exit.

The man looked disappointed, but not dismayed.

"Also hear you're not satisfied with the idea of an accident?"

"I am concerned that the cause of Steve's death be determined after looking at all the evidence and the circumstances. I was there at his cabin when Steve disappeared. I don't feel responsible for his death, but I do want to know what happened," I said, surprised at how easily I explained my involvement.

"I know what happened," the cowboy said. "Steve fell out of a boat in the middle of the night and drowned! Nora's brother supplied him with pot every time he came into town. Steve probably just took too much and lost his balance in the boat."

"Why would Steve go boating at night by himself on the lake just to smoke some pot?" I asked.

"You do ask a lot of questions, don't you?" the cowboy said, losing interest. "Look, everybody around here liked Steve. He was a great guy, always happy, always generous, never seemed to care what he spent in the terms of money. He was just a fun guy to hang around with. Steve was always helping out Nora's brother, if you know what I mean. Everyone knew Nora's brother always had a stash of pot available."

"Even the sheriff?" I asked.

"Sure," the cowboy said. "Even if the sheriff did decide to bust him on pot charges, later he couldn't. Bobby moved north of here and out of his jurisdiction."

"And what about Nora?" I asked. "Did she know all about her brother and Steve?"

"Of course. But Nora held herself in high esteem. Went to high school with Nora, I did, and she smoked pot herself then! But all Nora ever talked about was leaving this town. She used to hang out when she could with the tourists wanting to join their world...which she did when she married Steve. I'm still stuck here, and Nora's in the big city doing well, I hear. She never came in here with Steve. Too good for us now. Not the case with Steve...always the regular guy."

"Thanks for talking with me...got to leave and make some phone calls. Have a great evening. Sounds like the fun is just getting started," I said and managed to angle past him off the bar stool.

The man moved aside and started talking to another audience and was quickly drawn back into the crowd. I went to my room and called Nora.

I just wanted to skip Cabo, go home, forget all about these people and this place. But somehow, I knew I couldn't. Although I really hadn't seen anything, I believed Steve was killed, that it was neither a suicide nor an accident. I couldn't really rationalize my decision to stay any longer, but I felt compelled to see this through. I realized the next day was the beginning of Founder's Day Weekend, and Nora might come. She already seemed to know I was in Sugar Pine, but I wasn't sure how.

"So, you're still interested in buying the cabin?" Nora asked teasingly in that seductive tone of hers. "Is that why you returned to Sugar Pine?"

"Sure," I answered back, playing the game we both knew we were playing.

"Maybe you just wanted to see a small-town festival," Nora said. "It can be amusing. Gordon, Beth and her husband, Jim, and I are thinking of coming. Perhaps you could meet us Sunday night at the cabin after the day's activities for some snacks and wine?"

"I think I'll beg off, Nora. I don't think Gordon wants to see me again, and really I don't want to converse with him again either," I replied.

Nora just laughed. "Gordon can be quite burdensome, but he really has my best interests at heart. Perhaps you are right, Gordon might become angry all over again if he sees you. Maybe I'll bump into you in town anyway."

# Thirty-one

I woke up late the next day wanting something to eat before heading to town for Founder's Day. So, I got in my car, not feeling the need to exchange gossip with the oldsters at the coffee shop. I headed down the highway, hoping to find a different place to eat when I spotted a burger place I hadn't noticed when driving up here from San Francisco. It boasted a new sign and looked promising. Normally, I tried to stay away from fast foods in San Francisco, but now I had few choices and a greasy cheeseburger with fries sounded perfect. My diet had made a disastrous dive since being here.

The restaurant was part of a fast food chain and was emboldened with bright lettering with its logo and plenty of fliers on the windows and door depicting lots of calorie laden, juicy choices. I entered only to find out there was a line with several people waiting for service. From a few people behind me, I heard a man yelling out, "Say, you still owe me five hundred dollars."

I turned around immediately and saw a man about my age with long, dark hair that matched his beard which hung down from his face.

"My mistake. Sorry. You are not him," the man quickly apologized. "You look just like him from behind. My friend Karl has short hair, wears khaki pants and loafers and looks the opposite of me." Then he laughed a deep guttural laugh.

I don't think your mistake is funny, I said to myself.

"Do you know Karl?" the man asked, continuing the conversation which I wanted to end.

"No. Who's Karl?" I asked, wondering why I had bothered inquiring.

"Nora's stepbrother," the man answered, looking at the change he had in his pocket. "Don't know if you know her either."

My hearing perked up. I decided I did want to continue this chat.

"Actually, I do know Nora," I answered, "but I didn't know she had a stepbrother. I have heard a lot about her brother Bobby, however."

"Oh yeah, Bobby." He looked at me as I had turned around in line to face him squarely. The line hadn't shortened in the last few minutes.

"Bobby is THE bad boy of the family," he said. "Bobby is always in trouble. Karl is older than both Nora and Bobby and is the product of the first marriage of their mother. Karl is as cocky and arrogant as Bobby, but more subtle and clever. Karl's scams involve planning and carry-through while Bobby's efforts are usually spur of the moment and quick. Karl sets up scenes and plans for others to carry them out. They are white-collar crimes mostly, so he can't be easily caught. Pretty smart, actually. That's why he owes me five hundred dollars. Talked me into one of his scams. I heard Karl recently came back into town, and I would like to catch up with him." And with that remark, he made a strangling motion with his hands, and I got the message.

"If you see him," he continued, "tell Karl I would like to get in touch with him." He laughed at his own joke. "Touch with him, get it?"

"Who shall I say is looking for him?"

"Ted. Ted Owens." He tried to shake my hand, but by then both of us were holding money, which made such a gesture awkward.

Just then, the line started to move forward quickly and both of us seemed more anxious to get our order than to continue talking.

So Nora has a stepbrother, I mused. Interesting information.

Ted sat next to me at a table. I had no choice.

"Don't get involved with Karl," Ted advised. "Karl's a charmer. Can sell anything to anybody. Before you know what's happening, you're involved in one of his schemes. I should know." Then he munched on his cheeseburger hungrily.

"I have no intention of even meeting him," I answered. I pushed away the bitter coffee I had ordered. What I would give for a decent latte, I thought. Even a half decent latte.

"By the way you dress, and being an outsider, you are someone Karl would definitely seek out," Ted said with his eyebrows raised, and he smiled. With another munch, he made yet another comment. "Just don't get involved. Karl is always looking for someone to back him."

An idea popped into my head. "Did Karl have any dealings with Steve or his business partner, Gordon?"

Ted stopped eating for a moment and looked at me quizzically. "Could be," he said. "I hear lately Karl has gotten into drugs... marijuana. Even though it's legal now, it's still grown illegally without an expensive license. That would be just the deal he would like."

"What does Karl look like?" I asked. "Just in case I see him, I can avoid him."

"He looks just like you but with a big phony smile. Women are attracted to him. Stands out in a crowd because Karl is so outgoing. The type of guy you might spot as insincere if you were a cautious person, which a lot of people are not these days. Karl usually stays away from here because there aren't a lot of people with money he can prey on that don't already know to avoid him. But as I said, he has been spotted in town recently."

I had no more questions in mind, and Ted seemed to have used up all his information. There was something nagging at me in my mind, but I couldn't call it up until Ted left the restaurant. Did Ted know if Karl was a friend of the sheriff or did the sheriff know of Karl's illegal activities? Too late, Ted had left, and I didn't know where he lived.

I had eaten my meal much more slowly than Ted, and now munched away happy with my choices until I dropped some crumbs on the floor. After I reached down to retrieve them, I came up suddenly to spot a large red truck entering the parking lot of the restaurant. Anxiety gripped me, but I calmed myself and sank down in my seat. I fussed around for the notepad and pen I had with me and copied down the license number quickly before forgetting it. It seemed to be the same license number I had earlier recorded for the sheriff, but I wasn't certain. I reached over to the seat next to me to get my cell phone but realized I had left it in the front seat of my car. I cursed my luck. With only a few moments to decide what other action I could take other than calling the sheriff, I impetuously decided to follow the truck. I would follow it very slowly and not too far, but maybe I could at least know where it was headed and perhaps get a better description of the driver if he stopped again, perhaps for gas.

I believed the driver was too pre-occupied with snacking on his burger in his truck to notice me. When he pulled out of the restaurant, the driver surprised me by making a U-turn and heading back toward town driving north on Highway 108. Maybe he would stop at Sugar Pine. My hopes for this scenario dissolved when he drove right through the town toward Sonora Pass.

I dropped way behind him, but most of the other vehicles on the road exited at Sugar Pine. There was just one other vehicle besides ours on the highway by then. As we approached the turnoff to Bobby's cabin, I lost sight of him. But when I passed the turnoff, I spotted the truck slowly going down the dirt road to Bobby's cabin.

Must be one of his buddies, I thought.

I took advantage of the next viewing area and turned around to head back to Sugar Pine. Nervous, because the driver of the truck might only stop for a short while at Bobby's and turn around to return to Sugar Pine, I kept a close watch on the rear-view mirror to see who was behind my car. But after I passed Bobby's turnoff, my tensions eased, and I returned to Sugar Pine and my room at the inn without any further incident.

I couldn't decide whether to relate my spotting the truck and getting the license number to the sheriff. I knew he wouldn't appreciate my interference, but I decided I should contact him by phone from the safety of the inn.

"I thought I made it clear that you weren't supposed to investigate on your own anymore!" Frank shouted into the phone.

"I really wasn't investigating," I stated in my defense. "It just happened, and I didn't have my cell phone handy to call you."

"If Bobby has been somehow involved in all this, you could have been in danger just spotting him. His friends are not nice, especially with those that interfere in their business."

"What's next?" I asked, hoping to change the subject.

"Yesterday, I talked with the cranky, old guy that lives next door to Steve's cabin. He substantiated your statement about seeing Steve outside the cabin that night. Even though he is old, I do believe him. Seems sharp. I also contacted the owners of the other neighboring cabin, the one that is vacant. I warned them over the phone of possible burglaries, and they agreed to my giving it a so-called thorough inspection" for their benefit. Theoretically, it is available for sale, but because of the bickering amongst the family, the realtor can't really market the property," Frank related.

I know someone in the family who has been living there lately, I thought to myself but didn't share this information with Frank.

"What has Paul Smith, the insurance investigator, told you lately?" I asked him.

"You sure are pushy! Remember," Frank continued, "I am really not obliged to tell you anything, since you are not a relative. But I guess it is best at this point to keep you informed rather than having you running about on your own. I can tell you that Paul is really stuck and is hesitant to come to a conclusion. Paul doesn't know what to think, but he is still delaying the payoff on the insurance claim."

"Does he have a theory?" I asked.

"We both agreed that if it was an accident, it probably occurred when Steve was leaving for Baja with someone. It could be that Steve was running away from his financial problems," reported Frank. "We found two one-way tickets under his name for the following day according to the airlines when they checked his name against their records. Who the second airline ticket was for remains a mystery. Perhaps it was Nora, but she says not. She seemed surprised when we told her what we had found."

"So am I," I exclaimed. "Baja, California. What a coincidence. I was supposed to be in Cabo San Lucas this week myself."

Frank hesitated as if holding himself back from saying, "Why aren't you there instead of here?"

"What are you thinking?" Frank asked. "Don't get any new ideas. I have got to go now. I will see you at the festivities."

I left the inn and headed to the only wide street in town to watch the parade. As I looked around, I even noticed a few of the locals I knew and waved hello to them. I recognized the waitress and the old folks from the coffee shop, the bartender at the inn, and then I spotted Frank. He was at the head of the lineup for the parade and looked annoyed as always.

"Sorry I didn't tell you on the phone. Turns out you need to sign yet more witness paperwork from the other day. Julie is at the office now. See her first and then the parade, as she will leave soon to watch it. Everybody is here, as you can see, and most are in the parade. There is the high school band for music, the marching VFW guys, the local politicians in newly washed cars, and besides all that, we have a few homemade floats, pretty young Founder's Day princesses and queen and some horses. At the end of the parade is the town's volunteer fire department. There are lots of booths, but no Ferris wheel. Town couldn't afford it. All in all, it's spectacular for the size of our little village. Don't miss it on your way out of town," he said.

"Thanks for all the information. Is Nora coming?" I asked.

I don't know why I asked him that question, but if I wanted to get a rise out of him, I succeeded. He hesitated about answering, but eventually just turned and walked away. I guessed he had enough of me for one day.

I stopped by the booth featuring pine needle tea, and the young girl operating it knew less than I did about the process of making the tea. As I was paying, an older woman came to replace her, and she was surprised that I knew something about making pine needle tea. She and the local ladies club were in charge of the booth and had made sugar pine needle scones as well. She had some resin for sale and told me some people chewed on it like honeycomb. She assured me it was full of Vitamin C and I had to try it. I really didn't want to but felt I should buy some after chatting with her. The resin was sweet and chewy in my mouth, and I was glad I had been brave enough to actually sample it.

I watched the parade for a moment as the marching band from the local high school came down the street gingerly blasting out a tune. I always loved marching bands. Suddenly, behind me a hand moved across in front of me and grabbed my arm. Instinctively, I swung around ready to attack, although I knew I would be no match for a stronger man. I had no real fighting skills and had never been in any serious conflict. Nevertheless, I felt my muscles tense and my adrenalin kick in as I swung around to face my attacker.

"Don't hurt an old man," cowered Charlie as he seemed to shrink in front of my eyes.

"Shit, Charlie. You scared me half to death. I almost punched you," I yelled at him.

Charlie seemed to shrink and shrivel even smaller than his slight wrinkled build, and I began to feel a little foolish.

"Sorry, I guess I overreacted," I offered and gently took him by the arm to bolster him.

"You seem a bit on edge," he remarked quietly.

I let him go and he brushed down his shirt and pants as if to shake off the incident. "Geez," Charlie whimpered. "What's wrong?"

"Nothing," I said. "I guess living in a big city makes you cautious."

Charlie's wide eyes continued to stare at me, and I thought I needed to say something more.

"I guess Steve's death has spooked me. I can't get the sight of his body at the dam out of my mind."

"You saw him? After he died?" the old man quizzed.

"Yes, Steve was lying face down among the assorted garbage collected at the spillway, apparently a victim of drowning."

"Curious," Charlie said. "It was curious, you know. Wondered about it myself. Come on in for a moment. I have to sit down."

I hadn't noticed we were standing in front of his sign which read, 'Charles Evans and Son Auto Care.'

"So this is your store?" I asked him.

"Sure is," he answered. "Wanted to pass it on to my son. So when he was born, I bought this sign and proudly posted it. But my son has no interest in inheriting the business. To be truthful, he moved from town years ago—only visits occasionally. He's at the parade today with his family. We'll have dinner together later. Guess I just don't want to admit to myself that the shop will end with me. I probably should take the sign down and retire. Don't get that much business now, anyway. Sometimes villagers bring their cars by, and an occasional stranded tourist needs help."

Charlie offered me a chair, but I declined and remained standing. I didn't intend to stay too much longer. Wanting to change from this subject, I reminded him we were talking about Steve's death. "What was that you said about being curious over Steve's death?"

Charlie stroked his more than day old whiskers for a moment, as if to collect his thoughts, and then began a long dissertation. "I wondered about it when they told me about the accident. Everyone in town knew Steve didn't swim but loved fishing on the lake. Don't picture him going out on the lake alone at night."

"I didn't see anyone with him when he left the cabin," I answered.

"That's right. You were there the night he went missing," Charlie said.

"I saw Steve walk down to the lake. I thought he was just going for an evening stroll."

"Everyone in town liked Steve," Charlie mused. "He would visit the village whenever he visited the cabin. Easy to talk to, easy to gossip with, easy to be with. His partner, Gordon, was the opposite. Both were men of means, well dressed and groomed, but Steve was approachable. I only talked with Gordon once when he came to my shop with his fancy Mercedes. He needed my help as his car was making some loud noises when he drove. The way Gordon talked to me was condescending. Had I ever worked on a Mercedes? Had I kept up with these newer cars?"

"Gordon talked to me as if I only worked on old trash cars that the poor citizens of this quaint town could afford. Not only that, but he stayed the whole time I worked on his car, all the time looking over my shoulder loudly exclaiming, "Don't need to open the trunk. Don't need to.""

"I wouldn't have snooped in there anyway, but I did wonder what he had hidden in that trunk that was so important," said Charlie.

I wonder too.

"Nora's brother, Bobby, works on cars," I said.

"Hmmmm," Charlie uttered, stroking his chin again as if the wiry whiskers would help him think. "What a loser! I saw him talking with Gordon once in the street. Don't know what they would talk about anyway. They had very little in common."

"Those San Francisco folks. I didn't like them except for Steve. Too uppity. Too wild. Too everything. Nora was just as bad. Her brother Bobby was into drugs, you know."

I nodded. Everyone in town seems to know that, I thought.

"I had to fix his old truck a couple of times. When it really needed extensive work, I had to order parts. Otherwise, he fixes his own truck himself."

"Oh," I remarked blandly, not really interested and shuffling my feet as I was about ready to leave the shop.

"Bobby sometimes borrows Steve or Nora's truck when he does errands for them. They each have identical trucks, except Nora's is red and Steve's is black. Did you know that? Thinking it was cute, Steve bought them about two years ago at Christmas."

I abruptly stopped walking out.

"I didn't know that." On the night I arrived here, Steve parked his black truck in the driveway. Did I spot Nora's red truck following us on the highway? The sheriff had conveniently not mentioned Nora owning a red truck. I recovered my composure and wished him well. "Thanks for all the information. Have a good time with your family," I said as the bells jingled above the door on our way out.

"Thanks. I was just getting ready to go home when you came by. I don't think I'll do any business today unless someone's car breaks down and if that happens, they can call me," Charlie said, pointing to a notice on the door.

He walked down the street in the opposite direction of the parade, obviously not interested.

I strolled along toward the parade...thinking, and decided to stay in town a little while longer.

# Thirty-two

I had meandered further when I spotted Mrs. McGuire from the coffee shop scurrying down the street seemingly looking for someone. I tried to avoid encountering her and sought refuge, turning down one of the only corners of the short street and pulling my cap over my eyes as in a cheap mobster movie. But it was too late. She had spotted me and crossed the street as fast as a woman of her age could muster. Seems as if her eyesight was sharper than her hearing. I halted and waited for her. It seemed like the decent thing to do after my attempted escape.

"Oh, I'm so glad I caught you," Mrs. McGuire stammered between gasps of air, her wisps of white hair over her forehead beaded with perspiration. She stood for a moment regaining her composure, and as she stroked her bangs away from her face, announced the news which by now was not news to me at all.

"I wanted to tell you ..." she began and looked around to see if anyone was listening to our conversation. "Nora's brother was involved with drugs. Did you know that?"

I nodded when she made this statement.

Mrs. McGuire's face turned serious, and then the faint smile of conspiracy surfaced across her face.

Does she not know, I thought, marijuana was once illegal when Nora's brother was using and selling it back in the day, but it seemed the sheriff didn't really care anyway.

"You don't seem surprised," Mrs. McGuire said. She looked at me squarely with both hands on her hips. "Well, young man," the old woman said with a bit of Irish brogue accentuating her speech, "I am not just talking about soft stuff, but hard stuff." She lingered on the word 'hard,' emphasizing it.

"Bobby has made a living out of it. What I don't know, however, is where he got it from." She shrugged a little before continuing. "But I always thought somehow Steve was involved. And when the lot of them came up here from San Francisco, that would have been a good time for such a trade."

Now you have my attention, lady, I said to myself. Steve as well as Gordon could have been involved. Maybe Gordon's import/export business involved drugs.

Mrs. McGuire noticed my silence and the change of attitude that was beginning to show in my features.

"Well now, young man, you seem more interested," she said. "Of course it's all rumor...no hard facts, but it does put some ideas into what happened to Steve, doesn't it?"

I nodded and asked, "Did you share these ideas with Frank?"

Mrs. McGuire looked down at the pavement and spoke more softly this time. "Of course I did, but Frank didn't follow up on them. He could have been involved with them as well. After all, they were all friends at the time. I had better get back to the parade. I just wanted to tell you what I thought...in private...not at the coffee shop with everyone listening."

"Of course. Thanks for confiding in me. Have fun today," I said to her back as she ambled back to the street to join the others.

Mrs. McGuire had put some ideas into my head and now the circle of possible scenarios had enlarged, thanks to the town's gossip.

I followed her steps and when walking parallel to the parade I spotted a large black truck that looked like the same model as the truck Steve had parked in front of the cabin that first night.

What was it about trucks in the Sierras? They were all over the place. They seemed to be the normal method of transportation here, very unlike what was driven in San Francisco.

The ominous big, black truck was parked in the grocery store parking lot with no one inside. I debated with myself for a few moments whether to stand by it and wait for the owner or to return to his office and tell the sheriff. I decided on the latter and found him talking with someone on the street. The sheriff and I went back to the parking lot, but he was not happy about my intrusion.

"Maybe it's only Nora's truck. Since Steve's death, she has his black truck parked temporarily at the cabin. Maybe Nora was driving it. No mystery. We can check it out if only to make you feel better, and then maybe you will finally leave town. Lots of trucks in this town and they probably all look alike to you!"

Now is probably not the time to tell him Charlie told me about both trucks, I thought. By the time we got there, the truck and its owner were gone. We went inside the grocery store, but the clerk didn't know anything about either the truck or the person who owned it. He said there were lots of outsiders in the store and no one had asked for help to their car. It was a dead end.

"I should have stayed with the truck," I said.

"That's all I need is for you to wind up dead, too!"

We walked down the street and the sheriff headed in the direction of his office. I kept on walking and thinking. I concluded I should really apologize to the sheriff for interfering so much. So I walked back to his office. I walked past the window to the front door only to see Frank in an animated conversation with Nora...probably discussing her brother's death. I couldn't just stand there, so I walked past.

After the front door slammed, I saw Nora climbing into a car, not a truck. She was too absorbed in her own thoughts to notice me as she sped off. The parade participants still lining up gave her lots of room as they pushed back, obviously irritated at the reckless driver and the squealing wheels as she rushed past them. The sheriff, hearing the commotion, stepped outside his office and saw me.

"Not you again," Frank remarked in an irritated voice. "Julie said you hadn't signed that paperwork yet about the incident yesterday. You might as well do so while you're here. Now THAT would be helpful!"

The sheriff walked back to his small, private-office and slammed the door behind him. It was obvious he wanted no more of my help.

"Wow, he's really mad!" exclaimed Julie.

"What is he so mad about?" I asked hoping to get some information.

"Nora always makes him angry. Seems like they dated in high school, at least he liked her, according to the old guys down at the coffee shop," Julie said.

I wondered if Julie considered me an old guy. I was only a few years younger than the sheriff.

"Does Nora come into town often?" I asked, hoping to find out more about her visits with the sheriff.

"No, thank goodness," Julie said as she retrieved the paperwork on top of her desk. "Sign here. Are you leaving town now?"

"Want to finish looking around and have some barbecue first. It's a long drive back to San Francisco."

"Good," Julie smiled. "I will be at the baked goods booth later. Make sure you come by."

Julie seems to be flirting with me, I thought. Maybe she doesn't consider me an old guy. I sauntered out the front door feeling better. I headed down to the booths lining the sidewalk. I wanted some authentic small-town barbecue and, for whatever reason, wasn't quite ready to leave. Cabo San Lucas and Mexico were starting to enter my thoughts when I spotted a black truck which looked like the red one, but this time Jim, Beth's husband, was clearly the driver. I decided to follow him in my car. My curiosity has no bounds.

Jim looked irritated at not being able to negotiate the truck out of town easily because of the parade, which was in full swing. I took advantage of the opportunity and hurried to my car. Jim hadn't noticed me and, by the time I began following him, he had moved very little.

When traffic was allowed to flow again, I kept a short distance behind him. For once I was praising a traffic jam, and Jim continued driving the short distance across the freeway to the lodge where he parked, carried his groceries to a waiting boat at the marina, and motored out without looking back once. For whatever reason, Jim was in a hurry.

# Thirty-three

I rented a motorboat at the marina from a skeptical teenager who I'm sure was wondering why a single guy without fishing gear, no kids, and no supplies was motoring out on the lake. I didn't care. I wanted to follow Jim.

Jim motored north, straight to the end of the lake to the scores of cabins only accessible by boat. I hugged the shore, dodging in and out of the small bays, hiding in the shrubbery so he wouldn't become suspicious. Once I thought I had lost him, but I saw him docking the boat in front of one of the cabins. He was easy to spot, since tourist season hadn't started yet and only a few cabins looked occupied. Most were still closed from winter, with covered patio furniture and wooden slats protecting the windows. Quietly, I approached the cabin on the entry steps to the patio to hear loud voices inside. The window was open, and I heard his voice and that of a woman. I peeked inside. It was Nora.

"Did you talk to anyone? You shouldn't have gone. I told you so!" she yelled.

"No one noticed me. Everyone was busy with Founder's Day. No one would recognize me anyway," Jim said.

That's not true I thought.

"He does," Nora replied.

Does she mean me or the sheriff? I asked myself. When I tried to get a step closer, the old, creaky, wooden floor of the deck betrayed me, and I heard a cracking noise.

"What was that?" asked Nora. "Who could be out there?"

"Could be a raccoon," Jim said, but Nora knew better. "Raccoons usually look for food at night."

I didn't wait for any more conversation and possibly being found, and I walked as carefully and as fast as I could to the boat. When I got there, I decided to abandon it. There could be people on the trail, and I might be safer there. I headed back to the marina using the trail. I ran as fast as I could on the uneven, rocky path, hoping for another hiker, but it seemed everyone who was visiting Sugar Pine that weekend was at the Founder's Day celebration.

It was so quiet on the shore of that placid lake without a breeze, I could hear someone running after me in the distance, a fact that made me even more motivated. Jim wasn't a big man, but he might have a gun. At the moment, I wasn't thinking of that as much as falling. I stumbled several times but managed not to fall.

The cabin where Nora and Jim had been staying was located about halfway across the loop, so I figured it was about two miles to the marina. I realized I was out of shape and resolved in my fright to exercise more if I lived. Finally I came across a couple on the trail. They both were old, slowly taking their time on their leisurely walk.

"Hi there, folks!" I said breathlessly as I slowed to a leisurely pace. "Looks like I am not the only person who didn't attend Founder's Day."

I joined them and started talking to them even though they looked upon my intrusion with some apprehension. It was quite obvious they wanted to be left alone, but they were either too polite or too afraid to ask me to leave.

"We walk a small portion of this trail every day," said the old woman quietly as if to say someone knew they were on the trail that day.

"Me too," I lied. "I run it every day I come here, which isn't too often, so I am out of shape. Sounds like another runner is behind me."

Just then, Jim caught up with me and, looking at the situation, waved and kept on running which was disturbing. I walked with the couple as far as I could, but when the old lady indicated they were staying at the cabins near the beach with friends, I veered off. I decided it would be better to make it across the beach to the Lodge where hopefully there would be more people...younger, stronger people. At least a bartender might be there.

# Thirty-four

Jim discovered me at the bar and tapped me on the shoulder. I jumped back in alarm and spilled my drink all over the floor.

"Sorry I startled you. I just wanted to ask you not to tell anyone," Jim whispered in my ear and then proceeded to order me another drink and get a towel from the bartender.

I stared at Jim as I was on alert, expecting a struggle, but instead he surprised me and apologized meekly.

"I just wanted to talk to you and ask you not to tell Beth," he said.

"Not to tell Beth what?" I asked. "Not to tell her about killing Steve or Nora's brother?"

"What are you talking about?" Jim asked. "Steve's death was an accident and Nora didn't tell me her brother died. When did Bobby die?"

"Yesterday or thereabouts," I said. "Nora didn't tell you?"

"No, she didn't," and Jim backed away.

"What don't you want me to tell Beth?" I asked.

"Just about Nora and me," Jim said. "I thought you were snooping around and found out about us. Nora says you have been stalking her."

"I haven't been stalking her," I said lamely, not coming up with an excuse for why I was just spying on them. "How long have you two been having an affair?"

"I don't have to tell you that," Jim replied.

"Well, you're asking me to keep your secret, aren't you," implying he needed to tell me everything.

"All right, but you can't tell Beth. Nora and I were seeing each other before Steve's death, if that is what you are really asking," Jim offered.

"I am."

"How did Nora's brother die?" he asked.

"Bobby was shot," I said simply. At this remark, the man's whole body shuddered. After all, he is just a good looking professional from Marin County. Me too, I am just a financial consultant from San Francisco, I thought. How did I get mixed up in all this?

"Shot! Who shot him?" Jim asked.

"Don't know. That's what Frank is looking into. We found him in the mountains near Kennedy Meadows," I said.

"What do you mean, we found him?"

"I followed along with the sheriff," I said, not wanting to reveal all the details. Possibly Jim does not know about Bobby's death and, quite possibly, neither does Nora.

"And you said Steve's death might not be an accident?" Jim asked.

"The insurance investigator and the sheriff are investigating that still," I added, trying to shake him up further.

"Nora has said very little about an insurance investigator," Jim said.

This man either doesn't know anything or he is a great actor.

"I have to get back to Nora," Jim said.

"Better you just get back home to Beth," I advised.

Great advice, I thought. I still haven't gone home myself.

Jim appeared shaken, and when he left the bar, I ordered a second drink to calm my nerves and make plans. I would return to the inn, pack, and leave this place, never to get involved with these people again. This time I shall keep my resolve, I promised myself.

I decided I should say goodbye to Frank and leave on good terms, but Julie, who had not left yet for the baked goods booth, said Frank had gone home after the parade. Frank told her to call him if needed and that, in any case, he would return later that afternoon. I agreed the sheriff really needed a break. My disturbing him at this time was probably not a good idea, but I was determined to say goodbye.

I turned down his quiet street, void of cars, and situated mine behind the sheriff's jeep parked in the driveway. Probably everyone else was celebrating in town. After knocking on his front door a couple of times and getting no answer, I started back to the car and thought perhaps I should leave a note and glanced back over my shoulder. I noticed something odd, a shadow from a large object near the oak tree in the back yard. Whatever it was, it hadn't been there when I visited before.

## Thirty-five

Curious, I wandered to the back yard and spotted the red truck partially hidden by the house as well as some large bushes in front of it. I decided just to get out of there, when Nora appeared holding the screen door open.

"Come on in," Nora said in her most beguiling tone. "We weren't expecting you but do come on in anyway."

Nora was wearing the same outfit I had her seen her in earlier at the cabin at the north end of the lake with Jim.

Was she having an affair with the sheriff as well? Is this Nora's red truck?

As if in reply to my doubts, Nora opened up with some information.

"As you probably have already–heard, Frank and I knew each other as kids. I was just visiting him before I left town again, since I don't come here often."

Often enough, I thought, to stay in a cabin with Jim.

"Well, it's not my business anyway. I have to get back to San Francisco. I've been here long enough," I said.

"You have been here quite a long time, haven't you? I hear you have learned a lot during your visits."

I turned to leave, and she threw a last-minute teaser to hold me in a conversation. I was reminded of my ex-wife who used such a strategy when she wanted to get something from me.

"Oh, by the way...before you leave, Frank wanted to apologize for his behavior toward you lately. He really feels bad about it. Why don't you come in since you're already here?" Nora said, opening the screen door invitingly.

What a nice surprise – an apology from a sheriff. Who would think that would ever happen? A rather nice ending to this episode of my life.

I walked into Frank's house with Nora. As we entered, I didn't notice anything different. Everything was exactly the same as the day I had visited. The couch had the same tired afghan over the back, the rocking chair was in the same place, and the tall grandfather clock was ticking away against the living room wall. If they were having a torrid affair, they must have been frolicking upstairs.

Where was Frank anyway?

Nora answered my thoughts as I looked around the living room.

"Frank will be back shortly," Nora said. "He left with that insurance investigator who has been trying to make something out of Steve's death. That investigator has been quite a nuisance."

"So that is your red truck in the back?" I asked.

Nora seemed surprised at my comment, and she waited a moment before replying.

"Yes, but recently I offered it to my brother Bobby to use. He, in turn, loaned it to one of his friends for a while without my knowledge. I was upset by his actions, and I just got it back. The friend used all my gas, which further angered me. Why do you ask?"

"I think perhaps earlier the driver tried to run the sheriff and me off the road with it," I answered.

"My brother and his friends don't like it when the sheriff tries to investigate their drug dealings," Nora said, shrugging. "Sorry about that. Not my fault really. Say, I am going to have a beer. Want one?"

"No thanks," I said. "I think I should leave. I really don't want to wait for Frank. I need to get on the road."

"Oh please," Nora said. "I bought some fresh, homemade berry pie at the festival today. You should really try it."

"Okay, but I can only stay a few more minutes," I said as I proceeded to sit on the tired couch.

"Sit here by the end table," she said, indicating an upright chair by the old-fashioned swinging kitchen door. "It will be easier for you to eat the pie."

She disappeared into the kitchen and when I didn't hear from her for a few moments, I turned around to look for her. I was surprised to see Nora with a large pitcher in her hand standing directly behind me. I moved forward in my chair and stared at her.

"You are jittery, Matthew. I just thought you might want something to drink with your pie. Frank makes great lemonade," Nora said.

"I am sorry about your brother's death," I remarked, trying to regain my composure. Nora placed the lemonade on the table beside the chair and returned from the kitchen with a warmed piece of pie that smelled delicious. I was starting to forget about everything else with each bite.

"So you know about my Bobby's death, too," Nora inquired, pouring me yet another glass of lemonade.

"I don't know the details yet. Frank hasn't found time to tell me. Just said he discovered him near Kennedy Meadows. I suspect it was one of his drug friends who was to blame," she explained.

"Was that what you were arguing about with Frank earlier today at his office?" I asked.

Nora stopped suddenly and stared directly at me. "I didn't see you there," she said. Her voice had a strange pitch to it, and made the hair stand up on the nape of my neck.

"I was just walking by," I countered.

"Frank and I argue about other things," Nora said, putting her hand over her heart indicating a romantic relationship. "I guess he didn't tell me because he didn't want me to be too upset. Why else did you come here today? Have you forgotten to tell Frank something? You can tell me, and I will give him your message when he gets back."

I told Nora about our finding Bobby at the isolated lake. I left out some details except for my suspicions about the sheriff somehow being involved in all this.

"Oh, you are wrong. The three of us swam in that watering hole sometimes as kids—a long, long time ago," Nora said. "Bobby often camped near that hidden lake when he was older, and probably brought his drug friends up there as well. One of them probably shot Bobby over money he owed them. Sad.... Bobby never amounted to much."

"Unlike you," I replied.

At that last remark, Nora became quiet. "I hope the insurance investigator isn't meeting with one of my brother's friends for information. Bobby's friends can be dangerous. Maybe we should take a look in the truck parked out in the back and see if the man who drove you off the road left anything incriminating in it. It might help Frank's investigation."

Damn! She's holding me hostage here again with her latest ideas. I'm not interested in any of these complications anymore. I just want to go home.

"Oh, please," Nora implored, giving me that pouty look, manipulating me just like my ex-wife used to do. "I don't want to look in it alone. Just go with me for support and I'll do the looking."

I really have to get out of here.

"No, I said. "I just really want to go home."

Nora stared at me for a moment. Then she drew her body very close to mine. For a moment, I thought she might kiss me, but at this close proximity she instead made me a dare.

"Frank would help me if he were here at this moment. Are you scared?" she asked.

I am just as brave a man as Frank, I said under my breath. "I guess I can spend a few more minutes and help you out before he gets back."

# Thirty-six

We walked into the back yard. Since the truck was hers, I figured it was okay to look inside, but I was glad Nora was going to do the looking. I had no desire to be caught fumbling through the contents of the truck when Frank arrived.

"The truck isn't locked," Nora said, "so maybe the glove compartment isn't either. I don't know what his friends did with the truck. I haven't looked yet. We could get lucky. There might be some clues in it."

I watched Nora scramble into the front seat of the truck and open the glove compartment. How did she know the truck wasn't locked? Has she been out here before? The warning bells began ringing loudly in the back of my mind. Her frame blocked my view of the inside of the truck, and I was momentarily distracted by Nora's shapely body. But when she turned back to face me, I was frightened by her discovery of the contents of the glove compartment. Nora held a gun in her hand pointed directly at me.

"I did indeed find something in the glove compartment," Nora said nonchalantly. "I found a pistol."

"Please, put it down on the ground for now," I pleaded as Nora faced me directly. "We can show it to Frank when he gets here," I remarked as casually as I could.

"Why should I?" Nora remarked in a manner that alerted me to the fact that I should have been listening to my intuition.

"I intend to use the pistol...and you should be frightened." Nora wrapped her finger around the trigger like she knew what she was doing. And her hand was steady.

I was indeed frightened but managed to keep some vestige of calm in my voice.

"This is your truck and you drove it here?" I asked. Those warning bells were shrieking wildly. "Fool!" they shouted at me, "Falling for a line from a beautiful woman."

"You really should have stayed in San Francisco," Nora commanded, her mouth going ugly. "After you played your little part, you were supposed to return to San Francisco and never be seen again. But no, here you are. Your curiosity has caused me many problems."

The small-town girl who had struggled to become successful and who had climbed her way to the top by her resolve and her wits was pointing a gun at me. This Nora was determined to survive, and I had put myself at great risk.

"My part?" I repeated. "What are you talking about?

"Your part," Nora remarked coldly. "Steve and I came up with your name for the role you played in our little drama when we were planning it together."

"Steve and you?"

"Yes. Steve and I planned the whole charade. Gordon knows nothing about any of this. Foolish Gordon, my protector. When we were planning our little melodrama, Steve tried to recall old acquaintances who would agree to visit him here to become a witness to his so-called accident. Your name appeared at the top of his list. Steve uncovered your work week schedule and ran into you purposely at your favorite restaurant, which you so religiously visited on Fridays. From there it was easy. After taking you to lunch and convincing you of a possible job with him, Steve invited you up here to the cabin."

Shit! I have been such a fool to fall for all this. Now it's my turn to stall! The bore on the pistol aimed at my heart never wavered. "Who did I witness leaving the cabin at midnight?" I asked.

Nora smiled. "My brother bought an identical red plaid shirt like Steve wore all the time. What you saw that fateful night was what we staged for both you and Gordon to witness. Steve quietly joined Bobby at eleven o'clock at the boat dock after you and Gordon had gone to bed. Bobby and I led Steve to believe my brother was part of the scenario of a disappearance. My brother would meet Steve and take him by boat to the marina to meet me there, supposedly to leave for Mexico. Steve thought we were going to run away from our debts. That is why Steve withdrew money from the bank and bought two one-way tickets to Baja. My ticket was for a later time.

"Bobby was going to make good money for his assistance in our plan. But I devised a different plan for myself...one that would serve me better. My brother convinced Steve to smoke some of his pot in the boat on the way to the marina. Bobby laced the marijuana with something much stronger, and when Steve blacked out, my brother simply threw him overboard. Steve couldn't swim, as you as know, and so he drowned. The coroner was correct that Steve drowned, but it was Bobby who threw him overboard."

Nora threw these words at me, the pistol wavering. "Bobby walked back to the cabin dressed in a red plaid shirt to rattle the garbage cans at midnight just so you would hear him and think it was Steve going out the back door."

So Tom did see Bobby dressed as Steve coming back from the dock around midnight. All the information I had gathered was falling into place.

"Now you're getting it," shrieked Nora in a higher, more excited voice.

I think she is actually enjoying this revelation. Nora is almost bragging.

"You always assumed it was Steve who rattled the garbage cans on his way out the cabin that night. What you really witnessed was an illusion. It was quite simple really, and the plan should have worked until you meddled and ruined it coming back again and again. You were never satisfied with the idea of a suicide, or an accident. Now I have a problem and have to decide what to do with you," Nora said coldly.

"What about your brother Bobby? Did you kill him, too?" I asked. I have to keep her talking until Frank arrives.

"Bobby got anxious with all the meddling from you and Frank. He wanted to meet with me and argue about it. When we got together at the small lake where Bobby liked to camp, he became physical with me. His death wasn't really planned. We fought and I accidentally shot him."

"But it all comes out the same. Bobby's dead!" I shouted. "Frank should be returning any time now and you will somehow have to explain all this to him."

Nora threw her head back slightly and laughed again. "Frank isn't coming back. You just don't get it, do you? Man, you are so dense! I convinced Frank I needed help in the bathroom upstairs and when he was distracted, I hit him with a large vase I found up there. Frank is not coming to save your sorry ass."

I have been a complete fool. All I have accomplished for my meddling is a bullet with my name on it. My only hope lay upstairs on the bathroom floor. I am out of options! Life is too precious. I have to try to keep her talking until I can figure out something.

"Nora, you just can't explain away both Frank and my death at his house," I said. I am discussing my own demise, but talking with her and keeping her distracted is the only strategy I have left until I can think of something better.

"I honestly don't know yet, but I always manage to think of something. That is the only reason why I am hesitating. Do you have any suggestions?" she said, smiling into my face again.

## *Thirty-seven*

Out of the corner of my eye, I spotted Paul, the insurance investigator, walking slowly and carefully behind Nora. I tried not to look at him and keep her talking at the same time, but it wasn't easy. When Paul got closer behind Nora, he grabbed for the gun. Thankfully, the bullet meant for me went off in the sky.

I jumped forward to help Paul. He and I subdued her, but Nora was screaming all the way into the house. We found some duct tape and used it to secure her as well as her mouth. Nora just wouldn't shut up.

Paul and I found the sheriff upstairs, alive but unconscious, and I used my cell phone to call for an ambulance. After the paramedics left and the deputy took Nora away, I wanted to thank the investigator for being there at the right time for saving my life.

"Did you know about all this?" I asked him.

"I really didn't, although I wish I had," Paul said. "I really just came by to speak with Frank and ask if he had discovered anything new."

"Nora had me in her sights, literally, so I am really grateful you came. I really thought I was a goner," I said, patting him on his shoulder. There simply weren't enough words to express how grateful I felt. We left the house together and headed for town.

~ * ~

Later, when I visited Frank in his hospital room recovering from Nora's blow, I asked if he ever figured out any of this plot.

"Were you surprised Nora was involved?" I asked.

"I suspected her after the hike you and I took because of the area where we found Bobby's body. Only Nora, Bobby and I ever knew about that spot. I was about to investigate the full extent of her involvement. I was sure Bobby was involved somehow, but I hoped Nora wasn't part of Steve's death. I hadn't told you yet, but when I spoke with the old guy who lives next to Steve's cabin, he recognized a photo I showed him of Bobby. The old guy said he saw Bobby hanging around the cabin a couple of times and finally revealed that the very night Steve died, he had seen what he thought was Steve coming back from the dock around midnight. The old guy agreed it could have been Bobby dressed as Steve always did.

"I am surprised at how well Nora deceived all of us, including Steve, Jim, Beth, and Gordon. At the end, she was all alone in her deceit, except for Bobby, of course." Frank looked away, speaking softly. "I guess I let my past relationship with her cloud my judgment."

"Nora fooled the insurance investigator as well," I commented. "Paul knew something was wrong with the so-called events of the "accident," but couldn't prove anything. I think Nora would have been found out eventually, even if she had shot me," I muttered, still in shock over my near death.

Frank nodded. "We could have both been dead by the time Paul figured everything out. I think Nora would have simply fled after killing us. We were getting too close, and Nora, at that point, would have had to be satisfied with just getting out of a bad situation."

I shuddered at the thought Frank was probably right.

Frank looked down sadly from my gaze and pulled the blanket up closer. He looked sad and beaten down, not his usual forceful demeanor. Picking at the edge of his blanket, he continued pouring out his heart. "Nora always wanted more than she had at any time. A house in Marin, her own cabin here in Sugar Pine, and enough clothes for several women were not enough for her. Nora spent most of Steve's money as lavishly as he did. I think the plot was born out of desperation on both their parts. Poor Steve. He thought he was going off in the sunset with his wife. Apparently, Steve usually managed to get out of bad situations, but not this time."

Frank continued to lie against his pillows in the hospital bed looking gaunt and frail. Without his sheriff's uniform, badge and distinctive hat, Frank just looked like a middle-aged man, slightly balding, appearing more subdued and paler than usual.

I didn't know what to say to him. I mumbled something about my being a pest. Frank looked up, animated at last, and said, "Good thing you were. Nora might have gotten away with it if you hadn't been snooping around."

Then I guess Frank realized what he was saying and leaned back. "You were in the way a lot, that's true. At one time, I even thought you were involved."

"Me? I guess I did overplay my part. Nora probably wished she and Steve had never chosen me as a witness in their little drama. I was supposed to return to San Francisco and forget about the whole episode after Steve's death. I really upset Nora's plans."

I shuffled my feet and finally sat on the stool next to Frank's bed. I decided to stay a while longer and learn more.

"Too bad Nora never found what she was looking for out of life and, in searching, hurt so many people," I remarked, philosophizing just a bit. "I feel sad for Beth, too, whose life is changed as well. Even Gordon, who idolized and tried to protect Nora, will be shaken when he learns the truth about her. Although Steve involved me in his shady scheme, I feel sorry for him. It is a bit ironic that instead of him, I was the lucky one for once."

Frank looked at me as if he had a least one more secret up his sleeve. "You do know that Gordon is gay, don't you? Gordon just loved

Nora for what he thought she represented…good taste, good manners, and such."

I was surprised by that news but tried not to show it. I wondered if Frank knew that Nora was having an affair with Beth's husband, but decided against revealing this bit of information if he didn't know already. He felt bad enough as it was.

"Gordon will be heartbroken for he really adored Nora," Frank said. "So did I once a long time ago. Then, something in her changed and so did I."

After some more conversation, I left Frank with his thoughts about the past. I, too, was experiencing a multitude of different feelings. Fear had been the predominant one recently, but now I felt relieved. I decided to travel back to San Francisco that very day after saying goodbye to Frank. I realized I would never forget this incident in my life, but I didn't need to see anybody else involved in this tragedy ever again. The Sierras are incredibly beautiful, and I never did get the opportunity to finish the drive over Sonora Pass. But I don't think I will visit the Sierras again for a very long while. I have been given back my life, and Cabo beckons.

## *Meet Joyce Johnson*

Joyce Johnson has always enjoyed writing whether it be mysteries, poetry, historical fiction or children's stories. A resident of the Santa Cruz area for thirty years, she lives near the beach and is only hours away by car to the mountains of the Sierra Nevada. This ocean to mountain connection inspires her writing.

# Other Works From
# The Pen Of Joyce Johnson

***Highway One*** - Set in Northern California on the Mendocino Coast, it is the story of a young woman who housesits her friend's Bed and Breakfast only to be caught up in a murder.

***Final Voyage*** - A young woman books a cruise as a retreat from the drama of her pending divorce only to find herself a target of another cruiser at her dinner seating.

# *Letter to Our Readers*

## Enjoy this book?

## You can make a difference

As an independent publisher, Wings ePress, Inc. does not have the financial clout of the large New York Publishers. We can't afford large magazine spreads or subway posters to tell people about our quality books.

But, we do have something much more effective and powerful than ads. We have a large base of loyal readers.

Honest Reviews help bring the attention of new readers to our books.

If you enjoyed this book, we would appreciate it if you would spend a few minutes posting a review on the site where you purchased this book or on the Wings ePress, Inc. webpages at: https://wingsepress.com/